PRAISE FOR MONDO POTUS

"**M**ondo POTUS is the book I didn't know I needed: a satirical vision of an American future where an egotistical third-term president with hair that 'looks like a photograph of itself,' serving an outdated Constitution written in (oh my!) cursive, and a congress that resembles 'an unruly study hall' has re-made the country to his liking and finds himself in need of a presidential library. Enter the librarian to save the day in this smart and hilarious tour-de-force. David Hoppe's political insights are always surprising, his humor reminiscent of Vonnegut."

—SUSAN NEVILLE, AUTHOR OF *THE TOWN OF WHISPERING DOLLS* AND *SAILING THE INLAND SEA*

"**A**lready firmly established as a prolific playwright and non-fiction author, David Hoppe now adds speculative fiction to the mix, fashioning the tale of a not-too-distant future dominated by AI, the climate catastrophe, and politics-as-personality. Kind of like, um, now. Hoppe digs deep into his own library experience — as well as his encyclopedic knowledge of Hollywood film history — to offer a fresh, surprisingly affectionate and often hilarious take on the Trump era. It's effective therapy for the mere price of a book."

—JIM POYSER, AUTHOR OF *CLIMATE FOLLIES* AND *THE LAST ACTOR AND OTHER STORIES*

"Channeling the tone and tenor of the sailing master Donald Barthelme's mock documentary, *Robert Kennedy Saved from Drowning*, Hoppe is a true dead reckoner as well. Hoppe is our own Jonathan Swift of swift boating, our Skipper skipping stones on the opaque sidings of our glass houses. *Mondo POTUS* weighs anchor and lowers the boom."

—MICHAEL MARTONE, AUTHOR OF *PALIN AIR: SKETCHES FROM WINESBURG, INDIANA* AND *THE COMPLETE WRITINGS OF ART SMITH, THE BIRD BOY OF FORT WAYNE, EDITED BY MICHAEL MARTONE*

"Hoppe blends a deep love of language with an insightful, often humorous perspective. His compelling new narrative is thought-provoking and engaging, to the delight of long-time Hoppe readers like me."

—JULIA WHITEHEAD, AUTHOR OF *BREAKING DOWN VONNEGUT*, FOUNDER AND CEO OF THE KURT VONNEGUT MUSEUM AND LIBRARY

ALSO BY DAVID HOPPE

Letters from Michiana

Midcentury Boy

Personal Indianapolis

Food for Thought: An Indiana Harvest

With Van Kirby: *On the Table by the Window*

This book is a work of fiction. Names, characters, places and incidents are products of the author's imagination or are used fictitiously. Any resemblance to actual events or locales or persons living or dead is entirely coincidental.

© 2023 by David Hoppe
ISBN: 9798393135782

All rights reserved. No part of this publication may be reproduced or transmitted in any form or by any means electronic or mechanical, including photocopy, recording, or any information storage and retrieval system, without permission in writing from the author.

Cover art and interior art by Brian N. Berlinger
Book design by Andy Fry

First Edition

VICTORY DOG
BOOKS

CONTENTS

HOUR 1: (Intertitle) Somewhere in the South Atlantic 13
HOUR 2: A colorful swathe 19
HOUR 3: A prayerful moment 27
HOUR 4: I crumpled against her 36
HOUR 5: Graceland 46
HOUR 6: Bear air 51
HOUR 7: The not quite empty gesture 59
HOUR 8: Pretzel City, USA 69
HOUR 9: It floats 81
HOUR 10: Attacked! 95
HOUR 11: Supposed to be invisible 105
HOUR 12: People are trouble 117
HOUR 13: Origin story 132
HOUR 14: Maniacal zither music 143
HOUR 15: Incongruous small talk 150
HOUR 16: A notion, briefly 154
HOUR 17: Peace in the valley 164
HOUR 18: Hallucinogenic spritz 169
HOUR 19: (Intertitle) Somewhere in the Caribbean 182
HOUR 20: For lovers only 189
HOUR 21: Landfall 199
Acknowledgments 208
Collages by Brian N. Berlinger (1951-2022) 209
About the author 211

"The conception of people acting against their own best interests should not startle us. We see it occasionally in sleep-walking and in politics, every day."

–Richard Condon, *The Manchurian Candidate*

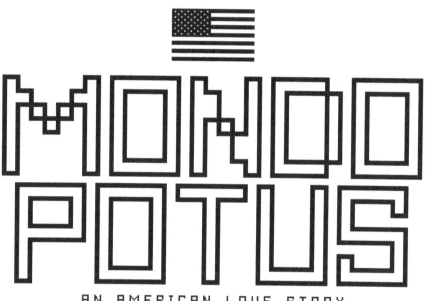

From WaPoLIVE:
Sept. 6, 2054
11:00 A.M. (EDT)

Mondo POTUS, the multi-million-dollar presidential entertainment center and library located aboard the former U.S.S. Gerald R. Ford aircraft carrier, has been reported lost in the South Atlantic Ocean. The ship sank at approximately 1:00 A.M. (EDT) on Sept. 6, according to a White House source. What caused the ship to sink, and why it was at sea just days before its official opening to the general public in Salty Shores, FL, are currently under investigation…

HOUR 1: (INTERTITLE)
SOMEWHERE IN THE SOUTH ATLANTIC

My name is Mutz. Duke Mutz. Two syllables, rather brusque-sounding, I admit. The origin is German; translated it could mean bear, like Smokey, Yogi, or the Chicago football team. It could also signify — and this is a little worrying — a docked animal. A puppy, for instance, the tips of whose ears and tail get cut off. Lambs' tails are docked, I've heard, because they do nothing but collect shit and attract flies.

Duke is my given name, not a title or term of endearment. It was my mother's choice. She was inspired by the Duke of Edinburgh, Queen Elizabeth II's imperious husband. Although born and raised in Hammond, Indiana, my mother loved the Royals. Their gentility, firm but modest nationalism, respect for tradition and, perhaps most of all, their accents, were like catnip to her. They had what she called "class." Funny, isn't? There was precious little class in her life. She raised me by herself, my father having flown the coop before I was born.

Did I tell you I was worried? Here I am adrift, sailing in automated circles aboard a floating mausoleum — somewhere in the south Atlantic. Although I have answered to many names in my time, sailor is not one of them. Fortunately, the ocean is calm tonight. If my luck holds, I'll have time enough to record this story before my wife's minions come to kill me. I figure I have maybe twenty-four hours. Like the song says, Love is Strange.

I told you my name: Duke Mutz. The date is September 4, 2054 and it is 11:53 p.m. Eastern Daylight Time. I am — or was — director of Mondo POTUS, the Presidential Library dedicated to POTUS's life and times. Mounting this massive tribute to the most consequential president since Lincoln aboard a former aircraft carrier (the beast I'm riding now) was my idea. We'll get to that.

As for POTUS the man, history — public or, for that matter, the personal kind — didn't matter much to him. The movies were his history books. That's why so many people thought a presidential library — for this president — irrelevant. His Kirk Douglas looks, torrential ego, the women, his progeny became part of the national dreamscape. By the end of his third term, POTUS was bigger than Mount Rushmore. Going in, my understanding of what a library dedicated to such a man might include was approximate at best.

Believe me, anybody who claims to know what constitutes a library today is looking in a rearview mirror. As Ranganathan, India's library guru, put it in his Five Laws of Library Science, a library is an organism that never stops growing. Libraries are malleable, subject to change based on whatever it is people want. I almost said, "what people need." But distinguishing between wants and needs is slippery, no? Telling people what they need, in this country, can get you lynched. Doesn't matter if you're right.

I wrote my Library Science thesis on Nadezhda Krupskaya, Lenin's wife. She championed libraries following the Russian Revolution. A photograph, taken when she was a young woman, shows a face no less beautiful for the earnestness of its expression. This, of course, was before the Czar was overthrown. Before the party feuding and purges. Before she grew heavy and wide — turning her body into her own personal bulwark in order to survive.

Krupskaya saw libraries as a way of keeping the revolution alight. The Soviet library system was her invention. In those days, the vast majority of Russians were illiterate. Given everything else they lacked, many people probably thought of libraries as merely ornamental. I mean people were starving! You hear something similar today — that libraries are irrelevant because all of us are carrying the equivalent of a big city Reference Department in our pockets. Even POTUS harbored (excuse the nautical pun!) doubts. He, by his own admission, never set foot in a library. "Why would I?" he asked me. "If I need something, I buy it!"

We weren't that different. Although the public library was a source of refuge and dreams for this fatherless boy when I was in junior high — my afternoons spent in the hushed, high-ceilinged reading room of our town's limestone Carnegie, poring over biographies of movie stars — I soon lost the habit.

I came instead to prefer the consumer-friendly browsing available in the bookstores I found in shopping malls. If I wanted a novel, say the latest by Ken Follett or Stephen King, I headed straight to Fiction. Books like *The Closing of the American Mind* and *The Art of the Deal* were, sensibly enough, in Current Events and Business. In these stores the covers were turned outward, like emblems of happiness itself. Browsing amongst them — grazing, really — came more naturally to me in bookstores than musty library stacks. Bookstores felt prosperous and up to date. Sexy. Libraries were for homeless people.

Thanks to Age Enablement I am considerably older than I look. I can remember what life was like before there was Income for All. In those days, if you weren't rich or disabled, you needed a job. It was called "making a living" for a reason. Without a job, you were nothing. Nobody.

A drinking buddy told me about Library Science. It seemed there was a shortage of librarians. Library schools were not only looking for candidates, they needed men. It was like "Surf City," that song by Jan and Dean (one of POTUS's favorites; he even sang it for me once, screeching the falsetto chorus: "Two girls for every boy!"). Reagan was president; government was the problem, not the solution. People wore parachute pants. Teal and magenta, those *Miami Vice* colors, were everywhere, along with cocaine, rightwing militias and AIDS. It was Morning in America. The end of New Deal politics. I wrote my Krupskaya thesis on an electric typewriter!

Free-wheeling cuts to public funding made employability in public libraries, even with my freshly minted MLS, more elusive than I had been led to believe. This, it turned out, was a blessing in disguise. It forced me to look for work in unconventional places. After a flurry of rejections, I parlayed my abiding love for movies (or cinema, the term of art at the time) into my first professional position: managing the Resource Center at the Center for Performance Art and Public Spectacle (CPAPS) in New York City.

I suppose each succeeding generation considers its early days in New York to have been the last best time to be there. The peak before everything went to hell. But New York's aura in the '90s was undeniable. If not as penny bright as the cast of *Friends* made it out to be, there was still a sense of opportunity bred by the promiscuous commingling of wealth and transgression.

Cheap flights to exotic places were so plentiful not a year went by without at least one airliner from JFK or LaGuardia crashing during take-off. Graffiti covered almost every public surface, from Harlem to the Stock Exchange and stickers advertising phone sex were plastered like smashed bugs to the plexiglass walls of city phone booths — before phone booths were obsolete.

Sex, as those stickers suggested, was everywhere. Looking back, it's easy to see why. Baby Boomers were in high rut. A generation that considered itself smarter, hipper, better was in charge, making fortunes, having its way. A Boomer, Bill Clinton, became President. He and a female intern famously used the Oval Office for intimate rounds of pussy play.

In those days it felt as if the sinews of New York's storied underground were knotted at my work place. Aging punks and toothless hippies, doddering beatniks and liver-spotted bohemians dating back to the Fluxus days used the place as a combination café, warming station and bathroom. They were, by turns, genteel, garrulous and crotchety. Occasionally, someone screamed. All of them had a claim on a version of New York that had been monetized out of existence. The lucky ones were memorialized in documentary videos and oral histories NYU media students produced for class assignments. We dutifully collected as much of that stuff as we could — so long as we didn't have to pay for it.

A few of these personages, like Yoko Ono, managed to become not just local characters but brand name celebrities. A fraction of them made financial contributions in order to keep CPAPS's lights on. Raising money can be a stressful, thankless job but in New York it puts you in touch with an otherwise unreachable class of influencers — the faces that used to be pictured dressily hobnobbing in the back pages of the *Times'* Style section.

For once my timing was opportune. High society was morphing into a playground where supermodels and entertainers — anyone who looked stupendous in designer clothes — were favored over old guard robber barons. Celebrities were taking over everything and, thanks to my movie crush, celebrities were my métier (or meat, as POTUS might have said). Before long I was dining on black beans and rice at the Dakota with Yoko, hanging in the studio with Isaac Miz and laughing at Woody's rueful one-liners at Elaine's. It was merely a matter of time before I shook POTUS's hand.

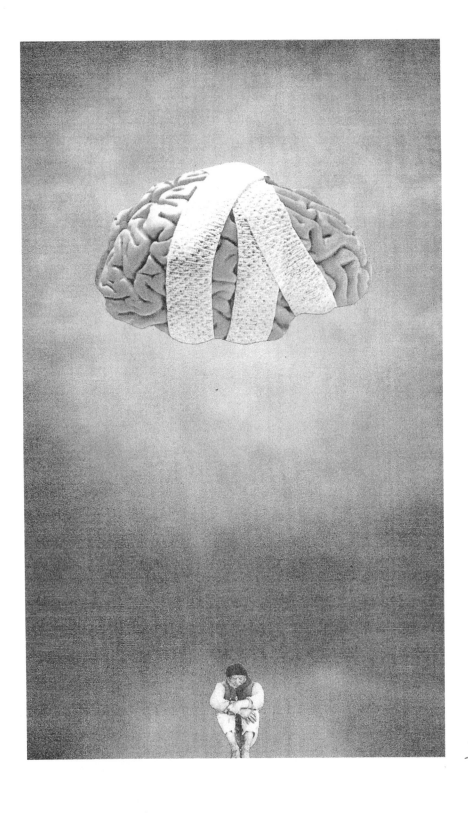

HOUR 2:
A COLORFUL SWATHE

How do I account for POTUS?

No one seems to care — which, come to think of it, explains everything. Whether you consider him an aberration, a visionary, or, as Del Capeheart had it, metaphorical payback for our country's self-serving way of confusing history with mythology, in the end POTUS was a fact. An exclamation point.

I first met him in New York. He helped underwrite an exhibition at CPAPS on performative consumption called "Existential Bargains." Our galleries were filled with multi-media installations encouraging people to imagine themselves as slave owners, big game hunters, Arctic explorers. My favorite piece was a pixilated space in which visitors were prompted to imagine they were making love with movie stars. Though the technology then was primitive, given to breaking up and fits of static, its arousal quotient was palpable. That said, I couldn't help noticing that visitors to the show were more interested in how this sort of art worked than what it meant. A foreshadowing, I suppose, of things to come. We arranged a private showing for POTUS prior to the official opening.

Both of us were chronologically younger. Me, trying to look shabby smart in a retrofitted '40s suit Robert Mitchum might have worn (the high waisted pleats, narrow belt and a vintage olive-crimson Countess Mara tie) and POTUS looking like the quintessential late 20th century Man About Town — decked out in branded opulence (Armani and Nike with a whiff of Jockey Club).

POTUS was reputed to be one of the richest men in town under the age of forty-five. The inheritor of radio stations in New York, Philadelphia and Boston, he transformed platforms that once provided Top 40 entertainment for suburban teenagers, into buzzsaws of white class consciousness, featuring meat-eating male voices growling on about how sick they were of liberalism, feminism and Chardonnay. He soon added stations in Chicago, Denver and Kansas City. Portland after that. Then Seattle.

It wasn't all politics. Sports talk became an even bigger jackpot. Sports and politics, POTUS saw, were underground springs feeding the same well. "Americans love their teams, us against them, winners and losers," he liked to say. Both tapped into a much deeper and abiding American loneliness. The yearning to belong. He hired on-air personalities who cut open the Big Game the same way his other talkers verbally disemboweled politicians and government. The modus operandi across platforms was identical: Fans and voters were amalgamated into a churning lump of grievance and nostalgia, enlivened by occasional flashes of celebration, like when a local team won the Super Bowl, or one of our guys put one of theirs in the hospital.

When we met, he was married to Wife #2. Juniper was a Brit, a sometime model, probably a heroin addict. She looked like a maple sapling with eyelashes. The three of us strode through the show as if we were on an urban safari, me playing Allan Quatermain (Stewart Granger's white hunter in *King Solomon's Mines*), POTUS and Juniper the aristocratic tourists looking to bag an exotic souvenir.

"Is this for sale?" Juniper wanted to know as we passed the lovemaking movie stars. POTUS took me aside, "Find out how much," he muttered, our shoulders brushing. It was our first touch of intimacy. The next day I relayed the artist's immodest price to POTUS who, after some ritualistic haggling, made the purchase — or said he did. The artist later filed a lawsuit for lack of payment.

POTUS's evasiveness with creditors eventually became a populist trope. Made him into a kind of rebel, someone for whom rules did not apply, rather than what was in fact the standard operating procedure of the very rich. I remember meeting an architectural photographer at the White Horse Tavern who told me how, after arriving at POTUS's country house to take a set of pictures of the place, he'd encountered a Latino groundskeeper cutting grass on a riding mower. The fellow mouthed the words, "Make sure you get paid!" as he motored by.

As the country straddled centuries, POTUS cut a colorful swathe through the rarefied social scenes of the larger cities in his media empire. Juniper became Giselle, who turned into Harley who was followed by Ava. Photogenic children, Luscious and Wilhelm, were born (to Giselle, an unsuccessful candidate for governor of Ohio, and Harley, who died prematurely after accidentally mixing a notoriously dangerous sleeping prescription with top shelf Mezcal). Meanwhile, their tycoon father's exploits on horseback, driving fast cars, and in the bedroom played across the pages of supermarket tabloids and celebrity magazines.

POTUS was the subject of a documentary on the sports network ESPN, featured on *60 Minutes* and given the chance to expound in a *Playboy* Interview. He presented himself as a distinctively American mash-up: aristo, entrepreneur, sex symbol and brawler. A man unafraid to give voice to the unmentionable, a slayer of shibboleths. "I'm like Oz," he dished to Whoopi Goldberg during one of her mid-morning TV gabfests, "except I'm happy to pull the curtain back myself."

He complained about his wealth without suggesting it was undeserved; lamented his tax rate without saying it was too low; admitted he bought access and influence in high places without proposing campaign finance reforms. Whether these utterances represented a critique of business as usual in our corrupt political culture, or the brag of a self-described winner was left for others to sort out. What became clear later, once he declared himself a candidate for President, was that his rhetorical flourishes were stratagems for finding public sore spots.

Hollywood played a part. I don't mean the faddishly liberal film community, but Movies, with a capital M. Only those who knew him well understood the extent to which POTUS was affected by films from the Golden Age. How when he was a boy he lay in bed, his face practically pressed against the screen of a portable Zenith TV, as westerns, pirate swashbucklers, historical fantasies and gangster melodramas drenched his brain. A carousel of American icons — Charlton Heston doing Andrew Jackson at the Battle of New Orleans; John Wayne being Davy Crockett at the Alamo; Errol Flynn's Custer fighting to the end in *They Died with Their Boots On* — made history come thrillingly to life. For POTUS, these movies amounted to a canon as elaborate and self-sustaining as anything imagined by the Greeks.

Flatterers learned the quickest way to turn POTUS's head was to liken the way he looked or carried himself to one of his cinematic deities: Jimmy Cagney, Bogart, or Cary Grant. But the Hollywood effect ran even deeper than that. It taught POTUS to experience the world as a linked set of stories, one bleeding into another, with an interchangeable cast of characters, like the repertory company at MGM, who were judged by their ability to play to type. I found it useful to model myself after Hoagy Carmichael's shrewd piano player in *To Have and Have Not* and *The Best Years of Our Lives*. You see, I knew old movies as well as POTUS did.

Over twenty years elapsed before our second meeting. I was in Los Angeles, working at the Yugen Endowment, a Japanese-American philanthropic foundation, known for its "Visionary" grants to "disrupters" in business, politics and entertainment. Our offices were located near the Pier in Santa Monica — body builders of all genders and Pacific Ocean glitter sparkled through my tinted, garden level windows. I loved the bare skin and technicolor light. The beach, that office, are under water now.

I managed the foundation's archive of products, media and related content produced by grant recipients, or "kulturonin," as they were called. Through a series of unanticipated (if all too common) events involving sexual misconduct, prescription drugs and an accidental death, I was soon promoted to Vice President.

Our board was keen to recruit POTUS. He was considered a catch, since he was hard to get. He rarely involved himself in philanthropic activity unless it provided an opportunity for self-promotion. When I mentioned our New York acquaintance to my superiors, they immediately put me on a plane to try and reel him in.

Our meeting took place in Palm Beach, Florida. He kept a super yacht on Lake Worth — a blindingly white, four-story craft the length of a football field. At sea, it looked like Mt. Fuji, a snow-covered peak set free upon the surf. "You like it?" asked POTUS, handing me a flute of diaphanous Dom Perignon as we took our seats on the sun deck near a diamond-shaped Jacuzzi. "It's the biggest yacht in the world."

I know now this wasn't true but it hardly mattered at the time. A glass-enclosed elevator had taken me to this height. It was the first time I had ridden an elevator on a boat; I thought it was great.

POTUS was not having champagne. Famous as he was for partying, he was one of those teetotalers who liked watching other people drink. His flute was filled with Martinelli's sparkling apple cider, which was topped and topped again by a steward in hygienically white Bermuda shorts whom I thought bore an uncanny resemblance to Gilbert Roland, the Mexican star of classic films like *The Bad and the Beautiful* and *The Gay Cavalier*.

POTUS wasn't interested in serving on the Yugen Endowment's board. "I don't play well with others," he said, arranging his mouth in that crooked, semi-self-deprecating smile of his. He launched into a lengthy, seemingly cordial, disquisition on his lack of regard for non-profit enterprise, explaining that he considered himself a "financial athlete," with a primal need for competition. "I mean, if I can't see a way toward beating the other guy, I have a hard time getting it up in the morning."

I wondered why he'd agreed to meet with me — still do. Most people want there to be reasons for things; that's why we find conspiracies so alluring. But sometimes there's no telling. Why something happens the way it does is unknowable. I think of what my life would have been like if POTUS hadn't taken our meeting. If I hadn't flown to Florida. And to think it all started with a work of art that made it seem like you were making love with a movie star!

"So," POTUS said, fixing me with an appraising squint, "you're in L.A. now." Off he went on a meditative jaunt, comparing life in Manhattan with the City of Angels. Weather and women. The latter, he concluded, were "drop dead gorgeous" in both places.

"Well," he concluded, staring at the sun, "I have to go now. The wife and I booked the Seafood Bar for a hundred of our friends. You should come. Their scallops are fantastic. I don't like scallops, but everybody says they're the best. Trini!" He called the steward, "make sure this man's name is on the guest list tonight."

POTUS's friends were packed like sardines into the Seafood Bar's galley-like space at the Breakers Hotel. After giving my name to a discreetly muscular factotum who checked it against a faintly glowing list on his electronic pad, I moved sideways, arms folded against my chest, toward the bar where I was told the evening's signature cocktail, the Luscious, was on the house. If I preferred something else, a Martini, say, or Manhattan, I would be charged as usual; mixed drinks started at $20.

I asked for a Luscious. It was golden with a swirl of green. Slightly but not too sweet, banked by a lingering note of heat. I was starting on my second when a mischievous female voice, gravely mocking, found my ear: "Do you really like my drink, or are you just a cheap date?"

POTUS's daughter, my cocktail's namesake, stood beside me, her blue, manga-sized eyes looming over the rim of a crystal Nick & Nora glass. Long hair, dark and accented by copper highlights, framed an already famous oval face. Her smile, to the extent she offered it, was white as photo paper, her teeth preternaturally large. I knew without thinking that my life's greatest opportunity was here.

My personal history of first meetings, going all the way back to junior high in Hammond, Indiana, is mostly (and mercifully) forgettable. The only constant being an attempted but not very penetrating wit coupled with the rather pitiful belief that amusing another person will make me, for a minute at least, worth talking to. Packed there, toe to toe, with Luscious in the Seafood Bar, this gambit felt, for once, like a waste of valuable time. Nakedness (or its rhetorical equivalent) was called for. Trying with all my might to keep my eyes fastened on hers, I told Luscious something that, even if it had never crossed my mind before, was true enough in that moment: "I have always wanted to meet you!"

She met this overhead smash with a deft backhand. "And why is that?"

My research kicked in. The tabloids. *People*. Wikipedia. I began mentally unpacking everything I had ever gleaned about Luscious's life, or what she almost certainly called her career: the sunglasses designs, her three-legged Rottweiler, championing clean protein ("eating Bison has saved them from extinction") and daybreak selfies taken in subtropical destinations during an array of moods. We talked. Or I talked about her, and she listened with mounting enthusiasm. It was as if she was a gymnastics judge at the Olympics, scoring my routine. Handsprings, scissors, saltos and twists: I watched the point totals mounting in her eyes. When she took my hand I knew I'd stuck my landing.

It was the start of an antic night. We explored the Breakers' endless hallways, back corridors and hidden recesses like a couple of urchins. We ran and skipped and snuck around corners. Luscious climbed aboard a serving trolley and I pushed her the length of a plush passageway, past snowy piles of discarded beach towels and trays of half-eaten room service. At dawn she led me to her suite overlooking the rumbling Atlantic Ocean. White-capped rollers followed one another up a sandy shingle of polished shells.

There was champagne. Luscious unsteadily poured from a pink bottle of Armand de Brignac Ace of Spades Rose. Its bubbles burst on my tongue like stars. We stood watching the sea for a while, letting our night's adventure settle. Then, without speaking or looking at me, Luscious placed her glass on the windowsill, reached behind her head and undid the tiny clasp at the top of her silk sheath.

"Unzip me, please."

She reminded me of Elizabeth Taylor in *Butterfield Eight*. I obliged — and there she was. Luscious in the flesh. Equal parts playground, rain forest and nuclear reactor. I should have bowed my head. Instead, I reached for the woman before me with both hands and, for the first time since we'd met, she went cold, turning from me slightly, just enough to create distance between us.

"Take off your shoes," she said — and I obeyed her. "Let's lie down."

She pulled back the comforter on the massive bed and the two of us made like mismatched spoons, the knit silk of my tie conforming chastely to the little Napoleon hats tracking down the curvature of her spine. As the day's first rays of sunlight opened up the sky, I closed my eyes and pretended to sleep.

HOUR 3:
A PRAYERFUL MOMENT

My name was one of the first things POTUS liked about me. Early on he seized upon the yin and yang of it, calling me Duke if something made him glad or amused and Mutz when he felt the media or so-called elites were out to get him. It didn't hurt that he assumed I was named after John Wayne, known to all who loved his movies, as "the Duke." POTUS insisted on this notion for as long as he lived, introducing me to everyone, from foreign dignitaries and oligarchic billionaires to crippled children and Venezuelan war widows as being, "my guy, you know, he's named after a movie star."

Not that I in any way resemble John Wayne. As POTUS's son Wilhelm, better known as "Billy," once hissed in a fit of sexually thwarted pique, I look like a "second string second baseman." I'm not sure if he had a particular player in mind, but comparing my looks to those of a light-hitting infielder is probably fair. Not bad for a librarian.

Ask anybody what a librarian is supposed to look like and the 1950s come to mind: a blue-haired lady, her glasses attached to a decorative chain, wearing a cardigan sweater and sensible shoes. I used this stereotype to my advantage. Made myself a pleasant surprise at professional gatherings. Luscious certainly liked me well enough. Billy, too.

Billy. Luscious introduced us. This was some time after our formative night at the Breakers and after I quit my job in L.A. to serve as Luscious's wingman cum "media advisor." POTUS began turning to me for "feedback" (eagerly given) regarding the organization of his monstrously overbrimming multi-media archive. There were storage facilities stacked with bankers' boxes full of clippings, photography, promotional materials and collectible knickknacks emblazoned with POTUS's name and face. I waded through a swamp of magazine covers, tabloids, videos (cassettes and discs), masses of audiotape, even oil paintings, trophies, and a cookbook featuring recipes for dishes I doubt

POTUS ever tasted, like Darjeeling Vesuvio and the cayenne-inflected Oysters Out Loud.

Billy had been abroad, trying to secure the rights to some coastal property in American Samoa for a real estate development aimed at retired surfers. He was sun-burnished and bearded when we met, wearing an adventurer's khaki shirt with buttoned epaulets on his shoulders. "Where there's a sand dune," he told me, "I see a dream."

As you know, Billy and Luscious were half-siblings, born of different mothers. Billy was slightly younger but more guarded. His father's success seemed to transmit a low decibel buzz, like an invisible dog fence, across the horizon of Billy's aspirations, intermittently jolting him into fits of paranoia and self-loathing. Cocaine didn't help. Nor did the frequent microdoses of LSD he hoped would rewire his brain and emulsify the shadow POTUS cast over his self-regard.

Sexual ineptitude didn't help. Unlike his dad, whose appetite amounted to a caricature of late twentieth century heterosexual bravado, Billy kept his preference for men on the down-low. Poor Billy. He seemed powerless to hide his attraction to me at first, a fact I realized could compromise me within the family circle. So I played dumb, pretending Billy's often ham-handed advances were his version of avant-garde humor.

Whatever dark spots his father imprinted on his psyche, Billy was mostly fine with being heir apparent to a media empire. And when POTUS vaulted over a scrum of boring candidates to win the first of his three terms in '40, Billy was at his side, smiling glassy-eyed into the mob of confetti-flinging fans. "Duke," he told me that night, sitting in his suite at the Willard Hotel overlooking Pennsylvania Avenue as car horns honked and throngs of drunken pedestrians staggered below us toward the Metro, "it's like having all our birthdays at once. This is the mother of all branding opportunities!"

We toasted our good fortune with an under-chilled bottle of Moet. Billy hugged me, put his head on my shoulder. "How does it feel, Duke? How does it feel to be part of — what do they call it? The royal court?"

"Fabulous," I said — and meant it.

"Because you are part of this. Hell, you have the name for it. You're a Duke!"

We both laughed and, gently but firmly, I made my exit, claiming to be exhausted though, in fact, I was late for an assignation with Luscious. Billy tried to talk me into going with him to the Lincoln Memorial. "C'mon," he pleaded, "it'll be just like *Mr. Smith Goes to Washington!*" I asked for a rain check and, much to Billy's chagrin, slid sideways out the door, which was when he compared me to a second string second baseman.

Luscious was standing beside her father in the hotel lobby. They were surrounded by an exuberant crush of backers and press people, all of whom appeared to be madly taking selfies. POTUS was trying to look cool, but the moment was too big, even for him. No one expected he could win the presidency. He was considered too brash and underprepared. Conventional wisdom had it that being a serial divorcee without a current mate would be counted against him. "Call me crazy," said POTUS — it became his tagline. We printed it on ball caps, pennants and business cards. The CMC belt buckle turned out to be huge with bikers and the pickup truck crowd. People took to saying "Call me crazy," instead of farewell or good-bye.

Down in the Willard's lobby, POTUS leaned into the wall of inflamed faces, pretending to listen to questions, nodding, laughing and greeting people he recognized as if they were his dearest pals. "Duke!" he beckoned when he saw me, "Get over here!" The crowd parted and I joined he and Luscious. Someone took a photo that was immediately uploaded to online news feeds: POTUS standing beside his daughter, almost cheek to cheek. My face appears in the little space between them, three-quarter profile, eyes averted. Trying not to steal the focus.

Suddenly POTUS turned his back on the mass of humanity in front of him, bringing his attention to bear on Luscious and myself. "I have an idea," he said. "Let's all go to the Lincoln Memorial!"

"Now?" Luscious sounded as if she had other plans. Or so I hoped.

"Now!" cried POTUS. "It'll be great. Like *Mr. Smith Goes to Washington*!" He addressed the crowd: "Who wants to go to the Lincoln Memorial?" It seemed everyone did. He looked at me. "Where's Billy? Get him!"

Going to the Lincoln Memorial on election night was like being in the eye of a patriotic hurricane. POTUS led a spit-polished three-car convoy on the brief drive to Mr. Lincoln's Greek Revival shrine. One after another, the cars pulled to a halt at the foot of the broad steps leading up to the enormous throne where Lincoln, gently glowing with overhead light, contemplates the country he sacrificed himself to save. Revelers, hammered by the climax of the nation's quadrennial frat party, skittered away from the headlights, only to freeze like deer as POTUS and his entourage (including Billy, looking like parchment, having barfed in the backseat of car #3) clambered on to the pavement.

POTUS paused to let the moment catch up with him. As a platoon of media commandos pushed and shoved their way into his peripheral vision, he put a hand on Luscious's slightly shivering shoulder and gestured toward the godly old man on high. "Look at that," he said. "It's like he's waiting for us."

With that, POTUS — with Luscious and downcast Billy trying to keep pace — ascended the fifty-eight steps to the memorial's great hall. Nixon, during the Vietnam War, made a pre-dawn visit here when, unable to sleep and reportedly drunk, he impulsively left the White House in a bleary effort to "rap" with anti-war protesters. The few he met said he talked about football and surfing.

Even though his face was red as a pickled beet and his knees, ruined from polo injuries, were firing angry bullets behind his eyes, POTUS made a point of not pausing on his way to the top. As he climbed, his face hardened. He seemed oblivious to the people grasping after him. When he made it to Lincoln's feet, he threw his arms around Luscious and Billy and they all bowed their heads, trying mightily to catch a collective breath. Hundreds of cameras flashed, documenting what looked like a prayerful moment.

A photographic mural of POTUS, Luscious and Billy, heads bowed, is the first thing visitors see when they cross the deck and come inside Mondo POTUS. It is roughly the size of a boxcar. POTUS loved it. "It's monumental," he cried. "Plus, you can see the Washington Monument in the background." True enough, the pointed little head of the Father of Our Country's phallic obelisk glows in the distance. This backdrop, combined with the explosive over exposure created by flash photography and the First Family's anguished faces, creates an effect both somber and sensational.

"It will blow everybody's mind," said POTUS.

Blowing everybody's mind would be his library's governing design principle. This brief was not unprecedented. Lyndon Johnson, the Texan made President by JFK's murder, added a theatrical touch of make-believe to his presidential library by creating a replica of the Oval Office at the University of Texas in Austin. The public enjoyed imagining themselves in the room where Johnson contrived to save Vietnam by destroying it. Public visits to the library soon outnumbered those by historical researchers.

Not surprisingly, Ronald Reagan's library in Simi Valley, the Los Angeles bedroom community where White police officers were acquitted after beating Rodney King, a Black man, to within an inch of his life, took presidential imagineering even further. Not content with recreating the Oval Office (officially described as the room in which Reagan "never took off his suit jacket"), library designers lured visitors to the Air Force One Pavilion, where they climbed aboard the actual jetliner used by the President. The New Deal wasn't the only thing Reagan dismantled. His library's foundation took apart an Irish pub he and Nancy once visited, carting everything but the locals back to California, where it was reassembled and repurposed as the library's café.

Bill Clinton's library featured an interactive quiz about 1990's pop culture and George W. Bush invited everyone to sit behind a pretend version of the Resolute Desk and play "the Decider."

POTUS visited none of these places. He claimed he didn't have the time. That job fell to me. I traveled the country, glossing the legacies of FDR, Truman, Ike and JFK. Wondered at how an accidental president, Gerald Ford, who served less than a full term before being dispatched by the mush-mouthed Georgian, Jimmy Carter, got not one but two libraries (in Grand Rapids and Ann Arbor).

I learned why people called excursions like these junkets, never failing to return to the White House bearing all manner of trashy keepsakes — the coffee mugs, key chains, commemorative plates, tie clasps and pen and pencil sets so many tourists crave. Whatever boodle I collected during these trips was displayed on a table in the West Wing with a sign for passersby to help themselves. Sure enough, by the end of any given day, everything was taken.

At first, having a presidential library meant little or nothing to POTUS. He preferred having an existing airport, one named after an historical figure no one remembered any more, like Chicago's O'Hare or Dulles in Virginia, rechristened in his honor. Even better would be having his name emblazoned across the marquee of one of the country's larger sports palaces. The problem there was that the home team needed to win at a rate impossible to attain without cheating. Someone (it must have been Veronica Tu) suggested creating a video game. This is currently in the works; a consumer model should be available in the Mondo POTUS gift shoppe — provided I don't sink this motherfucker first!

Where the library should be located was a riddle, since POTUS was a one-man melting pot, his ability to erase regional differences and characteristics being one of his greatest attributes. It was Billy who discovered Salty Shores. He had tripped to Florida for the dog racing in West Palm Beach along with Rocco and Benny, a pair of what he liked to call his "buddy guards." After trolling the gentleman's clubs near the airport in their rented Escalade, these would-be musketeers drove up the coast in search of breakfast. A sullen, empty stomach silence had begun to permeate the Escalade's leather-clad interior when, just north of Vero Beach, somebody sighted an exit sign for a Keke's Breakfast Kafe.

I can imagine dawn's marbled light illuminating the Atlantic Ocean's far horizon. The landscape at the edge of Keke's parking lot is a wheezy shade of blue. A white ibis pecks the ground by a dumpster. Extricating himself from the Escalade's back seat, Billy plants his feet on cracked blacktop and stretches, making a mental note of a plywood sign painted in an unsteady hand at the pavement's edge: LAND FOR SALE! 50 ACRES! SALTY SHORES TRAILER PARK.

He and his little band wolfed down a breakfast of banana split waffles, ham and coffee. Refueled, they piled back in the Escalade and Billy directed Rocco to drive toward Salty Shores. They came first to a narrow steel bridge. It spanned the intracoastal waterway and connected to a spit of land that was barely protected by a partially submerged breakwater — a detail Billy should have noticed, but didn't. A motley collection of small boats — owned, it turned out, by elderly Midwesterners — bobbed in rust-stained slips. At the entrance to the trailer park, a pair of gull-splattered mermaids, sculpted from poured concrete, rode what appeared to be broken-nosed manatees as if they were bucking broncos.

A few dozen trailers, some with flimsy aluminum carports attached, were anchored in tidy rows approximating a grid. Street names like Albacore Ave., Stingray St. and Bluefin Blvd. suggested a sense of place. Billy and his boys drove so slowly they could hear gravel crunching beneath the Escalade's extra wide tires. They passed a trailer painted red, white and blue with a U.S. Postal Service logo pasted on its side. A cardboard flap saying CLOSED hung from its weathered doorknob. The Town Hall was a pink fiberglass Quonset hut with a flagpole, corroded by the salty air, tilting slightly in front. Palm fronds rustled overhead and, a few blocks east, they found a splintered boardwalk crossing the hump of a sea grape-covered dune overlooking a tawny strip of beach.

An elderly man in a ball cap, his trousers rolled halfway to his knees, stood fishing by the water's edge, casting a long line into the ocean. Early morning sun made him look orange. When Billy, dressed all in black, with sand spackling his patent leather loafers, came up beside him, the fisherman flinched a little before looking down through the salt-occluded lenses of his plastic sunglasses. His name was Herman Schleisser. He, it turned out, was mayor of Salty Shores and, as Billy later liked to brag, about to become a millionaire.

In fact, everyone who owned a lot in Salty Shores became rich enough to buy an actual house somewhere well away from rising sea levels and hurricane landfalls. Billy happily told people who bought him dinner about his real estate coup. "Thirty acres of Florida oceanfront! Thirty fucking acres!" And POTUS, for once, made no effort to conceal the pleasure he derived from Billy's deal: "We can always do something with it if this library thing falls through."

HOUR 4: I CRUMPLED AGAINST HER

Here is something Luscious once said to me: "Why don't you take your clothes off and let me look at you."

When you are an Age-Enabled man like me, you wonder: Is this woman attracted to me, or is she merely curious? For those of us who are still working and can afford it, Age-Enabling makes a certain kind of sense. You're still in the game, you tell yourself. People see you and instead of yesterday they see today. But the memory lag — that feeling that what's happened to you happened to somebody else — can be disconcerting at times. I suppose it goes with this post-historical period we find ourselves in, where chronology becomes increasingly fungible. Time, it turns out, is not a railroad track but a kaleidoscope. It would be nice, though, if they could figure out how to make it so all your parts are affected the same way at once. My prostate, for example.

Luscious could have been my daughter — not that I thought of her that way. She was adorned in leopard print lingerie, complete with garter belt. We were in my apartment at the Dorchester; I had just returned from a library planning session at the White House. It was the third summer of POTUS's second term, a July so oppressively hot and humid tourists crowded into museums on the National Mall for the air conditioning.

We were making history. Luscious was enjoying her recent triumph over the Midwestern water rebels. Income For All, the guaranteed income bill, was on its way through an increasingly shambolic Congress (members of the various parties throwing crumpled wads of legislation at one another in the Senate, as if they were having a snowball fight). And we were finally about to scrap the Constitution. It was about time.

But here was Luscious. In my apartment. This was meant to be a surprise, though its impact was compromised by the Secret Service agents so obviously loitering in the lobby. Conspicuously adorned, as usual, with sunglasses and earbuds, they waited stoically, cracking their knuckles by the elevator and in the hallway outside my door.

Was it my birthday? No. A religious holiday? Neither Luscious nor I were members of any so-called faith community. Was the nation — the world, for that matter — on the brink of catastrophe? No more than usual. Luscious needed what she called her "me time" — the pronoun referring to her, not me, though I was the one she most often turned to for these interludes.

I'm not sure our relationship had deepened over the years, but it had certainly endured. Luscious loved turning me on. Though she was still repulsed by the exchange of bodily fluids, the wet and surrender of lovemaking or fucking — call it what you will — her ability to do this to me and my, I won't say delight, but readiness for what she elicited in me almost never flagged. There were times it made me confused and even a little sad. But, like the shipwrecked Robinson Crusoe, who prayerfully reminded himself that his glass was half full, I kept things in perspective. Luscious was not just any woman. And I was a patriot.

I say I was a patriot. I was employed! One of the lucky ones, or so I thought. Having been born long before social engineering like the guaranteed income came to pass, I was still acculturated to identify myself with where I worked and what I did for what used to be called "a living." That we, for generations, took this work or die approach to life, thought it was actually good for us, that people needed a job to get up in the morning, to feel their lives were worthwhile, and so on and so forth, seems incredible now. Thinking that healthcare depended on the kind of insurance employers were willing to provide seems downright feudal.

Not that POTUS was keen to send every American a monthly check. In truth, he hadn't really thought about it. Like most of us born in the pre-time, he considered amassing wealth the best reason for living. It proved he was better, smarter, more fit than most other people.

It proved he had taste — for what is taste but the ability to buy whatever is most expensive?

He had to be convinced a guaranteed payday was not an implicit critique of what wealthy people like himself thought of as the "work ethic." Members of the former Republican Party used to call tax supported handouts like this a disincentive. "No one will want to work," is what some suit with an expensive haircut would honk from the well of the House or Senate. POTUS's fears on this score were only allayed when he was shown how a regular check could take the place of the country's sclerotic social safety net. What's more, he was assured, a basic income didn't preclude anyone, like himself, from being rich or, for that matter, envying people who possessed great wealth.

The economy's semi-invisible hand ultimately pulled POTUS across the free-money finish line. The plain fact was there was less and less for people to do. Ultra-violet scanners told you why you hurt and whether it was worth fixing. Algorithms made legal cases to computers that relayed this information into overarching systems to achieve judicial verdicts. Data mining produced commercial strategies that once depended on human intuition, experience and creativity. Delivery trucks drove themselves. Robots called balls and strikes. As unemployment claims reached record highs it became easier for POTUS to pay people off than pretend somebody might hire them one day. "Your check is in the mail," became a national catchphrase that meant something positive for a change.

"Is it a library yet?" Luscious asked me as she lounged across the heat sensitive contours of my cine-comforter while I undid the buttons on my Nehru jacket. She was joking of course. The library was still in the task force phase. Architects, designers, scholars and, yes, librarians from across the country as well as China, the UK and Russia (reflecting my vestigial attachment to Krupskaya) had spent the afternoon brainstorming about what such a place might look like and the kinds of things it should include.

POTUS himself peeked in at one point, boyishly peering round the conference room door before making the fullness of his presence felt. After needlessly thanking everyone for attending, he made it clear he wanted his library to be something different: "I don't know what this is supposed to be," he admitted before adding with a hint of menace: "Do you? I hope so. We'll find out." Then he chuckled. "Like that judge said about obscenity: I'll know it when I see it." The assembled guests nodded humbly.

After the meeting adjourned, POTUS wanted to know if the heads of the Academy of Motion Picture Arts and Sciences Museum ("the Oscar Museum," he called it) and Disney World had been present. Yes, I told him, to the former, no to the latter. He chewed on this a moment, then changed course, as he was always wont to do: "There's a sex museum in Manhattan," he said. "Do you know it? I've been there. Saw an amazing exhibition on Japanese eroticism." I actually did recall the place, though I had never visited. "You know," POTUS continued, "they try to tell the entire story of sex. Opened my eyes." He then pointed to his eyes with the finger of one hand, as if pretending to blow his brains out. "Blew. My. Mind."

His conflating sex and museum-going was still under my skin, making me hot and bothered, as I arrived in front of my building and found a Secret Service agent waiting for me by the elevator. "Japanese eroticism," said POTUS, as if these words came as naturally to him as "medium rare" or "hedge fund." As I rode the elevator up, I couldn't keep myself from drawing pictures in my head of what an exhibition of Japanese eroticism might include. At CPAPS we had presented a performative installation by Daisetz Watanabe, a Kinbaku artist who tied women up in front of an audience. I was befuddled by how much his work aroused me. Naturally there were protests by women who claimed his work encouraged male violence against them. But while I sympathized with the protesters, I found something mysterious and abject in what Watanabe did. It seemed to me he deliberately upset the dynamics of sexual power; it was as though he was the supplicant and the women he tied up were forces of nature. The whole thing impressed on me how pathetic and lonely our received ideas of masculinity are. Sure enough, when the elevator opened at my floor, I was imagining Luscious elaborately bound and gagged, gently swaying from a chandelier in my dining room. By the time I entered the apartment, finding Luscious so fulsomely there, my breathing had quickened and my face was flushed.

Now I, to quote an old Kinks song about a transvestite, am not the world's most passionate guy. But Luscious in her skimpy leopard print get-up got me up. I flung my jacket to the floor and kicked off my shoes with such abandon one left a black scuff mark on the bedroom wall. Perhaps I alarmed her in some way, for Luscious's eyes widened as she pressed herself against me, whispering: "Was it Daddy again? Was it Daddy?"

I crumpled against her, plaintively nodding. Trying to keep up with Luscious's old man frazzled my synapses; not that I held this against him. He was so manifestly a genius. The richest, most successful guy I'd ever met. Luscious and I lay together, face to face on my bed and, like Scheherazade, she told me another part of her story.

I already knew that her mother (Giselle, wife #3) was a prosecuting attorney and a crack shot, a Midwestern horsewoman who met POTUS at a polo match in Wellington, outside Palm Beach. Her political aspirations drove a wedge between them. "It was always a power struggle," said Luscious, the fruit of that struggle.

Her mother was distant, as if she feared her daughter might siphon away the energy required to maintain her ambition. "There were things she wanted to do, things she realized Daddy made harder for her."

Luscious told me she there was little she could recall from her childhood. The years before she turned twelve were programmed as if they took place in a laboratory. A team of child developers groomed her to pass as a miniature adult. Giselle was absent, claiming her true self — her ambition, that is — could not be stifled. She opened a law practice in Cleveland representing recreational pharmaceutical manufacturers as the first step toward a gubernatorial run.

POTUS began bringing his big-eyed daughter to sporting events, opening nights and charitable galas. He got off on the attention the two of them received and Luscious went with the flow. It was all so bright and busy, awash with handsome faces, white teeth and amazing hair. Bad things (men could be so gross!) occasionally intruded but the flow never ebbed. Her days were nonstop. Luscious replayed everything she lived through in the privacy of her room, after her au pair tucked her in at night, scrolling through social media pictures and texts so quickly it was like whatever just happened to her had happened to someone else.

Luscious touched my face. "How was your meeting?"

"There were a dozen people there," I muttered. "They all had different ideas. Then your father walks in…"

"And throws everyone for a loop, I know," said Luscious. "But in the end, it doesn't matter what the others say. It'll be your call."

"Yes. But will I make the right call as far as POTUS is concerned?"

"It will be what he wants."

"And how will I know that?"

"I will tell you, silly!"

Luscious used her fingers to gently draw my eyelids down. As usual, what was inside me felt older than I looked.

The problem was ideas. The best architects had too many of them. They thought their job was to interpret POTUS — to himself and to the public. They arrived at the White House from offices around the world carrying great portfolios and natty little thumb drives bursting with drawings, diagrams, animations, photo-shopped illustrations and lists of key words intended to evoke all the qualities they thought a presidential library should project.

Some of these concepts were marvelous, genuine attempts to evoke POTUS's transformational impact on the presidency and the nation's history. I particularly liked what I saw by the Dutch architect, Woert, whose spherical model made of black, light absorbing hurricane-proof glass suggested a magic 8-ball.

But POTUS had his own ideas. Just as Krupskaya saw Soviet libraries as a way of permanently embedding the spirit of the 1917 revolution throughout Soviet society, POTUS, once he saw the project's trademark potential, wanted his library to not only enshrine and document his presidency, but confer a certain immortality. He compared it to Disneyland. "Mutz," he'd say, using the irritable tense of my name to emphasize the obviousness of what he was about to utter, "you think anybody would remember Walt Disney without the Magic Kingdom? Take away the theme parks and Mickey Mouse is the famous one."

Most presidential libraries are based on that most slippery of conceits, the public-private partnership. Ex-presidents create foundations to raise the money necessary to build the things; taxpayers generally cover upkeep. NARA, the National Archives and Records Administration, is in charge. NARA collects presidential papers and the vast amounts of commemorative trinkets, souvenirs and tokens of esteem — from guayabera shirts to cuckoo clocks — ceremonially collected during the course of presidential meet-and-greets.

Barack Obama did it differently. The Obama Foundation owned and operated the Barack Obama Presidential Center in Chicago. The foundation paid NARA to digitize everything — all the documentary holdings — for storage in NARA-managed records facilities located throughout the country. This freed Obama to tell the story of his presidency any way he liked, leaving NARA the humdrum task of playing umpire, deciding what and how to release presidential materials for research. The Obama library, in other words, wasn't really a library.

POTUS liked this approach. He bristled though at the government's claim on anything generated during his time in office. As far as he was concerned it was all proprietary material and he made good on his threats to block access to his papers through litigation. Many of those suits are still pending, even though POTUS himself has, as they say, left the building.

He fancied himself a storyteller in the tradition of classic Hollywood. His life, he believed, should be presented as a ripping yarn. He considered his lucrative conflation of sports and political analysis, turning citizens into fans, akin to *The Adventures of Robin Hood*. His way of using sex to tickle the public's imagination was, he said, inspired by Dean Martin's portrayal of a truant lounge lizard in *Billy Wilder's Kiss Me, Stupid*.

Assembling the POTUS Foundation wasn't hard. Oligarchs from around the world practically lined up to donate cash. We had two billion dollars in the bank before there was a sketch of what POTUS's library might look like. This made me anxious. If you think working for such a spontaneous man helped teach me to manage my fears, the opposite was true. For him to be spontaneous, I had to be structured. Not only that, I needed to anticipate whatever was coming next.

I worried. It's what factotums do. "Worry well!" should be our motto. Worrying is also part of every librarian's DNA. The work is about details, nothing but. When you think about it, getting the details right — making sure Philip K. Dick precedes Dickens on the Fiction shelf — sums up the librarian's trade. Unless, of course, your library still reserves a special section for what we used to call Science Fiction.

I met with Luscious and Billy in the White House bowling alley to discuss my concerns about the lack of a concrete library plan. Nixon installed the bowling alley — just one lane — after finally getting himself elected in 1968. It's a charmingly kitschy midcentury gem, reflecting Tricky Dick's relentlessly suburban sensibility. The dusty pink walls are lined with stylized images of giant bowling pins, the gutters are a polished baby blue. It was Billy's idea to meet there; I would have preferred a bar off Dupont Circle. But Billy was already lacing up his red, white and blue pigskin bowling shoes by the time Luscious and I arrived. A trio of psychedelically marbled bowling balls awaited us. Luscious, in form-fitting slacks and heels viewed the balls with dismay.

"Billy," she groused, "don't expect me to play."

"C'mon," snarled Billy, "change your shoes."

As the oldest one there, I felt the need for some kind of decorum. I took a seat and slipped out of my Italian loafers by way of making peace. Billy made no secret about feeling burned by his father's impending decision to cast Luscious as his third term running mate. It wasn't that Billy coveted the job. No one, including Billy himself, thought he was qualified. Not intellectually. Not emotionally. Apart from scoring the site at Salty Shores, Billy's ability to get anything done remained, at best, a dubious proposition. His snit was sibling rivalry, pure and simple.

Luscious glanced in my direction and, sighing, began to change her shoes.

"Look," I said, as Billy lifted a ball marbled with purple swirls, "we need to get to first base on the library project. POTUS keeps saying no to every architect we've introduced him to. But he doesn't give me a clue as to what he really wants. Whenever I ask him, Disney is all he says."

Billy gathered himself and rolled a strike, the pins exploding like thunder in a lumber camp. He suddenly looked a couple inches taller. "Disney, eh?" he murmured, daubing his fingers with hand sanitizer.

It was Luscious's turn. She cradled her ball in both hands and pigeon-toed it to the line. The ball crashed halfway down the lane, rolling harmlessly into a baby blue gutter. "He does this all the time," she said. "It's his way of avoiding commitment. He's afraid of making a mistake. I don't think the architects you've brought in appreciate his greatness."

My ball looked like a melange of pea soup, yogurt and peri peri sauce. I knocked over three pins on the left corner and missed the spare.

"I think he wants to be in control," said Luscious.

"What else is new?" said Billy.

"But he also wants a great building," I said.

Billy rolled another strike. This one made the titanium in my dental implants hum. "Eliminate the middle man," he said as he sat beside me.

"Just what I was thinking," said Luscious, who appeared ready to agree to anything if it meant she didn't have to hoist another bowling ball.

"Have a Designbot do it," said Billy.

"That way Daddy can say he did it," chimed Luscious, "which will, I guess, be true. Technically speaking."

"More work for you, of course," Billy looked me in the eye. "Since the old man's never going to figure out how to program a Designbot! But nothing you can't handle, Duke. You're a librarian."

Luscious patted me on the arm. "Just make sure there's a members only champagne bar. Plenty of parking." She wasn't joking.

But Billy laughed, "I can see it now. This is going to be the first presidential library with a drive-in movie theater."

That's what I was afraid of. By coming up with their DesignBot idea Billy and Luscious figured their work was done. *Deus ex machina*, emphasis on the *machina*. Their faith in technology betrayed an innocence I found exasperating. This was a generational difference, I suppose. The difference being that where Billy and Luscious believed in technology, I was still enamored with experts. A sex therapist programmed my virtual porn! Instead of a DesignBot, I wanted a design whisperer.

HOUR 5: GRACELAND

Though not yet a brand name in her field, Veronica Tu was building a reputation for coaching high asset clients intent on building dream homes (and thinking they themselves designed them). "I play well with others," she liked to say, a heart-shaped smile popping the features of her moon-shaped face. I liked her. When I spoke, she leaned in to everything I said with an avidity that evoked empathic professionalism. POTUS's library, she suggested, could be a kind of dream home, like Elvis's Graceland, only more so.

Veronica had done her homework. Knew POTUS loved Graceland, had made the trip — a kind of pilgrimage, really — more than once. He and I used to talk about it. "You can have Monticello," POTUS told me. "Graceland is this country's ultimate house." He squinted, as if trying to transport himself there, to the Jungle Room with its shag carpeting and built-in TV screens or the Meditation Garden, where Elvis's body was buried. "You can still feel his presence. It's like he's upstairs, watching his favorite shows." According to POTUS, Elvis invented modern America. "He's our Zeus, right down to the lightning bolt: Taking Care of Business in a flash!"

If POTUS had previously seemed distracted or less than enthused by the prospect of his presidential *library*, Veronica Tu's allusions to Graceland put a newfound light in his eyes. When she said, "It should be equal parts *Viva Las Vegas* and *Jailhouse Rock*," POTUS could barely contain himself. One afternoon I walked into the Oval Office to find him watching Elvis's *Blue Hawaii*. "Looking for ideas," he said, hastily changing the channel to a live Senate hearing on the implications of climate-induced mass migration to the Midwest. It was the first time I had ever seen him appear furtive, which gave me a little boost.

I soon came to see Veronica's Graceland idea as liberating. I understood Graceland. It was all about canonizing Elvis as a secular saint,

Saint Elvis. Saint POTUS had a ring to it! If Elvis was the first rock and roll superstar, you could say POTUS was the first rock'n'roll president — not because he was a rock music fan; he wasn't. His taste in music, as far as I could tell, revolved around Henry Mancini's movie themes: *Breakfast at Tiffany's, Charade, Experiment in Terror.* POTUS rocked because he was an ahistorical disrupter, the front man for a country hooked on performative highlights. Like the time he wore combat boots and a holstered .45 to peace talks with the Venezuelan Prime Minister. Or when he greeted the press with a comic shrug in Stockholm the morning after bedding Crown Princess Gudrun (half his age!). Our country, in its demented dotage, craved an older guy with the scent of reckless youth. Our job, I thought, is to package this.

I met Veronica Tu for brunch at the Cosmos Club, a venerable insider's hangout near Embassy Row. It took me all of POTUS's first term and half the second to tease out a membership, but it was worth the wait. The CC effectively evokes a more serious, more ambitious Washington, D.C. A time and place where earnestly dressed and well-connected men could meet beyond the vulgar reach of partisan politics to affirm each other's prejudices and worldliness, patch up differences and keep the country safe for free enterprise. It was, as far as I could tell, the only place left in the city still requiring neckties. I would not have been surprised to find Teddy Roosevelt lingering in the reading room with a glass of port.

Veronica and I were allied by mutual need. I needed her to coach me through the process of designing POTUS's building. She needed me to make sure POTUS approved the outcome. She greeted me in the CC's drop zone with a snappy salute, "Good morning, teammate!" Substitute "comrade" for "teammate" and Krupskaya would have saluted back.

We both ordered aqua-farmed shrimp cocktail. The brawny chunks of horseradish in the sauce made our eyes well up so that it seemed for a moment we were weeping together. That was funny. It promoted what I guess you'd call a bond between us. Once we'd wiped away the tears and could actually converse, I got the sense Veronica thought my relationship with POTUS invested me with powers I did not actually possess. I made no effort to disabuse her of this notion. I liked being thought of as the inside guy, a 21st century iteration of FDR's fixer Harry Hopkins (albeit without Hopkins' grotesque stomach cancer). She wanted to know how we met, what I'd done BP — Before POTUS. She told me she had never thought of librarianship as being a science.

"Tell me about yourself!" I magnanimously changed the subject.

Like almost everyone I seemed to meet, Veronica was years younger than myself. It was her bad luck to come of age when the bottom finally dropped out of higher education. Hers was a familiar story. She was halfway to her architecture degree at the University of Pennsylvania, when the university, under-enrolled and groaning with debt from having built a new student mall and three new stadia (including the first domed cricket arena in the MidAtlantic states), declared bankruptcy. She spent a year tweaking online menus for a chain of Indonesian carryout restaurants before persuading her parents to pay for a Designbot bootcamp. The bootcamp took six weeks and was half the cost of an undergrad semester.

"I'm a building whisperer," said Veronica, making the machine-tooled cardboard bracelets on her wrists snap like a shuffled deck of cards. "AI can design a building that works, but it still needs inputs. A sense of purpose. That means articulating in a way that is economically expressive what the client — in this case, POTUS and, when you think about it, the people of America — wants. Want. Whatever."

"One and the same," I said, as if talking to myself.

"One and the same!" Veronica lit up. "That's right! Have you been to Graceland?"

"Once," I said. "I found it very moving."

"I was amazed by how sexy it was," said Veronica. "For something so old. Still hot, smoldering, right? Because Elvis's taste was never predictable. Not that he was experimental or avant-garde. It was more like he took common fantasies and pumped them up, made them bigger, brighter, shinier than most people dared imagine by themselves. POTUS is like that."

I hate asking people in these situations who they voted for. One of my best kept secrets is that the last time I voted, it was for the elfin Texas billionaire Ross Perot in '92. He was cranky and comical. I thought Veronica and I were establishing a little rapport here and I didn't want to derail it. But my unwritten job description included making sure that anyone with access to POTUS was a loyalist. This became standard operating procedure during the first term, before POTUS recreated Washington in his image. Although there were plenty of qualified people — in civil service, business and what was left of academe — few could be trusted. At least not as far as POTUS was concerned. This changed, of course, after the landslide following his second campaign. The third term was still to come as Veronica Tu and I cleared our sinuses over shrimp cocktail at the Cosmos Club. In any event, when I finally asked Veronica what box she checked in the last election, she treated it like a batting practice pitch.

"HIM! Was there anybody else?"

"Just checking," I laughed, to make it seem like I was joking.

"You know I didn't vote in the first election," Veronica confided. "I wasn't registered."

"Most people weren't."

"But then I didn't feel like voting expressed my true self. I mean voting is a form of self-expression, right? And since nobody running looked or acted like me, I didn't care if I voted or not. I shouldn't have been so superficial, but I was young! Once POTUS was elected I saw the light. He really turned me on."

I couldn't help smiling.

"What?" She pressed me.

"You're very disarming, Veronica."

"There's no blah-blah with POTUS. He doesn't tell me to do my part, go out and save the world, be part of something bigger. POTUS tells me, everybody, we're fine the way we are. That's Call Me Crazy, right? But you know this. You've known him for years."

"I have known him for years, it's true."

"Don't you love him?"

"I owe him," I said. "I owe him everything."

Veronica nodded, licked those rosy lips. "That's the same thing, isn't it?"

We heard the honk and cry of sirens. They were in the background, then they became abruptly present. Men at nearby tables dropped their napkins and got quickly to their feet. Veronica and I followed suit. We became part of a small crowd moving toward the dining room's entryway. I'm tall enough that I could get up on the balls of my feet and see over the heads and tailored shoulders of the bureaucrats in front of us; Veronica, who was short, stared into their backs as if trying to divine what was going on.

An ambulance and fire squad were outside in the drop zone. The cherry blossom sunlight Washington, D.C. is famous for (but all too rare these days) made the whirling emergency lights seem much brighter. A couple of doormen, wearing their anachronistic double-breasted club uniforms, stood by, trying to look useful as First Responders carried an inflatable gurney into the building. I overheard a man I recognized from the Commerce Department ask a doorman what happened.

"Secretary Pompeo had a seizure in the weight room," said the doorman, referring to the former Secretary of State. "Somebody said he was triple-vaxed this morning at his doctor's office. Must've had a bad reaction." The man from Commerce accepted this without comment. We caught a glimpse of the former Secretary, swaddled in inflatable pillows, being hustled down a short flight of steps. His head was thrown back and the Age Enablement had drained from his face. His complexion was gray and what little hair he had left looked brittle. As the First Responders hoisted him into the ambulance his eyes fluttered and he managed a yellow smile.

HOUR 6:
BEAR AIR

Unlike me, blabbing into the void while this massive boat I'm sitting on turns circles atop a whispering ocean, POTUS was not a confiding type. You didn't see him sitting side-by-side on the monogrammed upholstery of Air Force One, whispering into somebody's ear. Despite what historian Del Capeheart dug up about him, I believe there are things we will never know about POTUS. One thing I *do* know, however: He took a long time in the morning. "Duke," he once told me, "never hurry in the morning. That's the secret."

The consensus among Wives #1 through #5 was that POTUS was a light sleeper. After making love (as per Ava's memoir) he would drop into an alarmingly deep slumber for about forty-five minutes. Then come to attention, wide awake as an eleven-year-old playing flashlight tag. This did not mean his amorous battery was recharged so much as that he was ready for more general sorts of action. Executives responsible for his holdings in different time zones grew used to receiving emails, texts and even phone calls at hours usually reserved for the deepest dreams.

This ability to eschew the seven or eight hours of sleep required by most mortals was, in POTUS's estimation, one of the characteristics of supremely successful people. He liked to quote Keith Richards to the effect that his lack of shuteye meant he'd lived twice as much. He rejected the phenomenon of jet lag, claiming he could set his biological clock like a watch for any time that suited him. Like so many CEOs, he ordered caffeinated Diet Coke by the caseload.

Nightowlishness aside, it was not uncommon for POTUS to fall into a second sleep shortly before dawn — a trait he shared with Dracula. Mind and body would topple as one down the well of his consciousness, finally settling at the silty bottom until roused by his valet at 6:30. If he dreamt during this time, he claimed not to remember.

He preferred a sparkling Martinelli's over orange juice for breakfast. What was it about his appetite for carbonated sweetness? If it's true there's a crime at the heart of every American fortune, I suppose an arrested adolescent is probably lurking there too. It must have been the bubbles. He needed something to chase his usual eggs, sunny side up, three strips of bacon and jellied white toast. POTUS ate like a chubby kid on vacation. Though no one dared tell him, it showed by the second term, when his fitness regime seemed mainly to consist of stress and insomnia.

He took three hours to ready himself when he was at home. Sometimes more. Rees Maudlin, the Irish Prime Minister, was kept waiting past noon while POTUS mulled over which tie to wear with a chalk stripe suit. He'd shower for half an hour, running the water from hot to cold. Then he sat on the toilet in a kind of meditation, during which he practiced the abdominal flexes he swore reduced the risk of hemorrhoids (for which he had a deep and abiding aversion). "You need a good shit in the morning," he told me with unfeigned seriousness. "It centers you."

POTUS shaved using a boar bristle brush and a psychopathically sharp straight edge razor. He favored Geo. F. Trumper's shaving creams, imported from London and set each morning in a mahogany tub on his wash basin. He shaved himself, pulling the skin taut along his cheeks and chin, dousing himself afterward with a florid splash of neon green Caswell-Massey Jockey Club cologne — reportedly JFK's favorite.

Unguents, salves and powders were applied. There was a painstaking routine with a pair of ten pound dumbbells involving a sequence of lifts and stretches punctuated by periods of rhythmic breathing. As time consuming as these rituals were, none was as deeply considered as the daily styling of the President's hair.

An Executive Scalp Therapist was on daily call. She (of course) entered the living quarters an hour before noon every day but Sunday. Her routine included massaging POTUS's tender follicles, making sure they were sufficiently moisturized, applying topical nutrients and trimming as necessary. Not since Reagan had the presidential hair looked so like a photograph of itself. POTUS maintained that being well groomed helped him concentrate.

He summoned me for a meeting the day after my Cosmos Club lunch with Veronica Tu. I was instructed to be in the West Wing at 12:30, which meant we probably would not be face-to-face until at least 1:15. To my surprise, however, he came striding down the hall at exactly the appointed time, with Luscious and Billy in tow. His cologne (powerful notes of musk and tonka) enveloped all of us like fallout from a flower bomb. As usual, his coiffure was perfect.

He greeted me as Duke. Always a good sign.

We proceeded to make ourselves as comfortable as we could in a room where minions who pretended to be invisible took miles of notes and photographs. Luscious and I sat at opposite ends of a chesterfield sofa, facing Billy across a glass-topped coffeetable. POTUS occupied a dark green leather chair with copper studs. He played host: "Does anyone want coffee, sparkling water, anything?"

When all three of us demurred, saying we were "fine," POTUS looked upward, as if addressing the ceiling: "Diet Coke, Rodrigo. Please."

He turned his gaze on me. We were getting older, but you'd hardly know it. When you've been working together with someone for years, you cease to notice changes. Age Enablement made it feel as if the two of us were the only still figures in a time lapse landscape where everything, from the weather to traffic to other people, passed us at light speed.

"I wanted to meet because I've seen a couple stories about my library in the media," he said. "The boo birds are already taking shots. They claim my library's not serious. There won't be any 'scholarship.'"

"I'm so glad we're doing this through our own foundation," said Luscious.

"Fuck 'em if they can't take a joke," piped Billy.

POTUS chuckled benevolently. "You're right, Wilhelm. Obviously. But I don't want this sniping to spook potential funders. We aren't going to pay for this ourselves, God knows. And while I don't care what the so-called historians say, there are a few investors, er, donors out there who might be concerned about how this looks in terms of its potential earnings. That's where you come in, Duke."

I nodded. Wore my best Man of Few Words expression. This kept me in good standing with POTUS. Before, when he was merely rich and powerful, not yet Leader of the Free World, we reached an understanding that still held between us.

We were in Chicago for a football game between the Bears and Las Vegas. The game was on a Sunday night; it was damp and dark, a penetrating wind coming off Lake Michigan. The Bears' stadium, Soldier Field, was by the water's edge. When this old shrine to the war dead was renovated at the beginning of the twenty-first century, misplaced frugality combined with Midwestern masochism — pride in watching a mediocre team play in barbaric weather — convinced planners that adding a climate-controlling dome was unnecessary. Season ticket holders paid top dollar to boast through chattering teeth that playing in "Bear weather" provided their team with a competitive edge. Sitting there, exposed to the elements for the hours it took to play a game, was promoted as a provincial rite of passage.

On that night in Chicago there was a lot of chumming among the cohort able to afford the warmth provided by corporate skyboxes. The owners of both franchises craved personal time with POTUS. His sports media empire helped keep the masses of fans unable to buy tickets for these headbanging bacchanals emotionally invested in "their" teams. Boys and girls were taught the value of loyalty at an early age by parents and grandparents spinning yarns about feats by beloved players who, for a few seasons, wore the uniform of their hometown franchise. POTUS's sports network amplified these stories to mythological proportions, providing platforms where fans devoted themselves to the painstaking analysis of coaching decisions they would never make, skills they would never possess and outcomes they would never affect. Sports talk, you see, became the template for our political discourse.

Being in Chicago was a homecoming of sorts. Being from Hammond, just over the state line in Indiana, I was practically a Chicagoan, a denizen of that amorphous metro area popularly known as "Chicagoland." The railroad made Hammond possible; there were more train tracks running through the place than Frankenstein had stitches. It was a steel town, where even blue skies looked gray. The people were Eastern European, African American, Latinx. When I was growing up, it was a labor union stronghold. Working hard was valued more than working smart. Now Hammond is another suburb, albeit built on hazardous waste. I was plotting my escape from there before my voice changed.

Accompanying POTUS, I tried to present the streetwise attitude I grew up associating with the Windy City. Incorporated what I hoped was a Sinatraesque swagger to my step. This vibe came naturally to POTUS. He flirted with the owner's wife from the Vegas team and ate ribs without using a knife and fork, licking the sweet and spicy sauce from his fingertips. We were there to celebrate some Chicago Bear anniversary; I don't remember which one. The mood in the stadium, packed and celebratory at the game's beginning, grew sullen toward the end, as cold permeated the concrete and it became obvious the Bears were going to lose.

POTUS hardly noticed the crowd's mood. That's the thing about skyboxes. They're a world apart. You needn't watch the action on the field; you can follow it on an oversized screen. Conversations take place with no one getting hoarse. There's real silverware; the napkins are made from Egyptian cotton instead of recycled paper. Sound dampening pile covers the floors and no one wears an overcoat. As Vegas ran out the clock, POTUS leaned in my direction and said it was time for a walk.

"I need to pee," he told me as we hit one of the enclosed concourses. The crowd on the polished concrete boulevard was thin. Many had already started home. We strolled briefly, feeling the great space above us, hearing subdued heckling from disappointed fans in the background. POTUS was favorably impressed by the stadium's indoor amenities, like Bear Air, an organic mood altering aerosol system that scrubbed the building's oxygen supply and infused the place with the subliminal aroma of grilled salmon. "Makes me hungry," he said.

We swung right, into a white-tiled comfort room. Although a far cry from days of old, when men lined up at steel troughs in a ritual of communal exposure designed to enthrall and intimidate children (and not a few of their fathers), public lavatories remained a challenge for contemporary designers. After passing a wash-up lounge where half the motion sensitive sinks were marked OUT OF ORDER, we entered an incongruously bright yet cavernous space with a long line of porcelain urinals built into the wall on our left. The swinging doors of toilet stalls on our right hung open like the mouths of fish. Secretly relieved that we appeared to have the place to ourselves, I decided to use this opportunity to jettison the ungodly payload of bbq pork, Polish sausage, French fries, coleslaw and beer rampaging through my gut. I ducked into a stall as POTUS, his back to me, faced the wall and began unzipping.

My pants were down around my ankles when I heard scuffling and a raucous male back and forth ricocheting off the massive tile surfaces outside my stall. Then a pregnant pause.

"Well," I heard someone growl, "look at this!"

"Hey," echoed a second, even hoarser voice.

"I know you," drawled the growler.

POTUS, I could tell, was speaking over his shoulder: "I don't think so."

"Yeah," cried the growler, his voice multiplied by the hard, ceramic, almost empty space. He laughed: "Man, what a tiny dick!"

"Very tiny," giggled the second voice.

"Hands off!" cried POTUS.

My sphincter tightened like a plastic pair of zip cuffs. I pulled up my pants and wobbled to my feet. Ordinarily, I am not a demonstrative guy. Physical courage has never been my strong suit. When I was a kid in working class Hammond, I dealt with blue collar bullies by acting so spastically crazy punks derived no pleasure from beating me up.

Nevertheless, I managed to fling open the stall door with such force it sounded like a cannon shot. I then launched myself toward the man I took to be the growler. My closed fist connected with the side of his head in a hammer blow, or what I've heard more physically experienced men call a sucker punch. Its impact was such I couldn't tell what gave way first — my knuckles or the soft part of the growler's skull. He fell to the floor like a dynamited high-rise. His companion, a scuttling blur of blue jeans, parka and averted face (glasses, I think) beneath an orange knit cap emblazoned with a blue Chicago 'C,' got the hell out of there.

POTUS, still unzipped, appeared to be what the media likes to call "visibly shaken." He was wide-eyed and his hair mussed; he looked like a traumatized owl. Both of us instinctively turned our attention to the man on the floor. He was bundled in the kind of puffy yellow jacket favored by construction workers. The guy was big — taller than either of us — with a curly head of graying hair, a walrus mustache and salt and pepper stubble. Thin strings of bright red blood trickled from his ear and nose and puddled on the floor. Although he looked as still to me as a forgotten load of laundry, POTUS insisted he was breathing.

POTUS blinked and zipped his pants. My hand felt like a sack of pain. I began to tremble. POTUS said: "Let's get the fuck out of here."

I waited in the gangway outside the owner's box, cradling my swollen hand like it was a baby. I could see POTUS speaking with the Bears' president, a man everyone called Booger. Booger put a commiserating palm on POTUS's shoulder and POTUS nodded in my direction, saying something with what looked like great seriousness. Booger nodded emphatically and reached for a phone. He touched POTUS's sleeve apologetically. POTUS shrugged. "It's taken care of," he said when he joined me. "A doctor will meet us at the hotel. Can you make it?" He patted me on the back. "Sure, you can."

In the years that followed, neither of us spoke about our Chicago trip. I don't know, but it is possible I got away with murder that night.

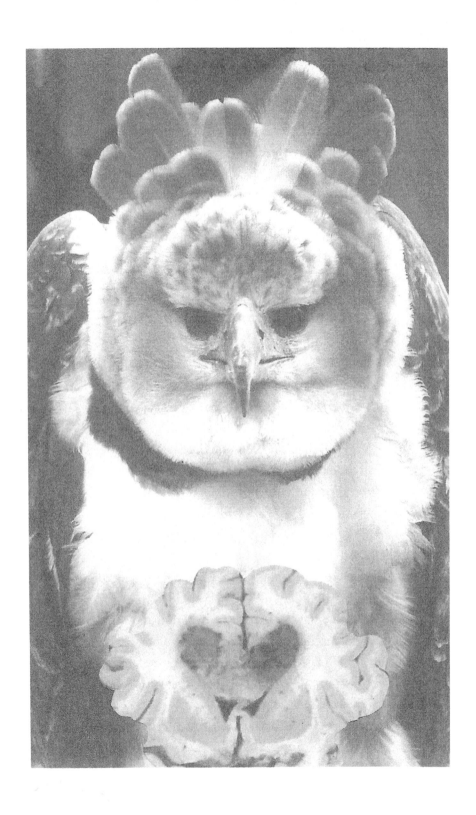

HOUR 7:
THE NOT QUITE EMPTY GESTURE

Sitting beside me in the Oval Office, Luscious was speaking about the library: "It's got to be an experience. Like being wrapped in goose down."

"Like being in the Situation Room," said Billy.

"Like performance art," said Luscious. "Right Duke?"

"Sure," I said, turning to POTUS, "We want people to feel what it's like to be you."

What did POTUS want?

"The movie of my life," was the most helpful thing he said that day. All of us, Luscious, Billy and me, knew what he meant, although in differing ways. Neither Luscious nor Billy had the background I did with classic Hollywood. For them, movies were necessarily in color, with super heroes and bombastic special effects. Stars that looked like catalog models.

But I knew that, deep down, POTUS retained an almost childlike affection for b&w melodrama: *The Bad and the Beautiful. The Magnificent Ambersons. The Letter.* Movies with faces that showed a formative viewer what grown men and women were supposed to look like.

Think Kirk Douglas's film producer (like I said, a not unreasonable POTUS facsimile) in *The Bad and the Beautiful.* He's a manipulative cad, willing to betray his friends in their most vulnerable moments to get what he wants more than anything else in the world: another box office hit. When he calls his oldest collaborators together to help raise the money for a comeback film, they make a show of turning him down. But his energy is viral. The movie ends with everyone eavesdropping on an extension phone, enthralled, as Douglas pitches his latest dream.

Remember the scene where Douglas carries a blacked-out Lana Turner in his arms and drops her in a swimming pool? It reminded me of POTUS's first campaign. That time he yanked the little American flag pin off his lapel in the final debate with McLemore. Nobody but John Birch Society types used to wear those pins when we were kids. But after the 9/11 attacks in 2001, every politician in the country, from the President to the county coroner, was obliged to stick one on their chest. Those pins became as ubiquitous as the logos race drivers plaster on their fireproof suits. McLemore made the mistake of calling attention to the little flag, trying to make some point about his love of country and traditional values. POTUS practically leapt on him. Called wearing a flag pin "a low bar for patriotism," before tossing the one he was wearing into the audience like it was a guitar pick at a rock concert. Political operatives all over the country gasped, but the crowd in the hall applauded for over a minute — it felt like a generational shift.

That's when I fully grasped the power of POTUS's instinct for the not quite empty gesture. Something that stirred people up but required nothing in the way of accountability. I don't know if he planned on throwing his flag pin away that night. If so, he didn't say. No one — none of the hyper-educated managers, pundits and pollsters who hang around campaigns and shape the conventional wisdom would have advised him to do it.

But POTUS knew how to read a room. He also read McLemore, an earnest striver, who confused worn out generalities about how "hard-working" and "innovative" and "big hearted" Americans were with the reality on the ground. POTUS made a fortune investing in Americans' appetite for celebrity gossip, pro sports and porn. He understood in a way McLemore couldn't that, deep down, Americans were haunted by the knowledge they could never have the kind of life they fantasized. Though it hurt too much to say so, most Americans had seen enough to know they were losers. McLemore trying to tell them otherwise — thinking this was "leadership" — only made them bitter.

Throwing away that lapel pin was electrifying. *Call Me Crazy* in real time. It showed POTUS wasn't afraid to make his own rules. Voters liked that. Of course, we made sure to have buckets of flag pins available for free at every rally after that. In a weird way the flag pin became our campaign button. People started wearing them to show their support for POTUS's candidacy. We keep a supply in a Stars'n'Stripes bucket on the counter by the cash scanner in the Mondo POTUS Gift Shoppe. If this barge ever makes it back to land, they will sell for five dollars apiece.

In thinking of POTUS's life as a movie, we began by assembling a family tree of visual landmarks, like the flag lapel pin. We also drew on film and video archives, holography, still images and animations. Veronica Tu even commissioned a painting — a faithful reproduction of Emanuel Leutze's "Washington Crossing the Delaware," with POTUS's face inserted where Washington's used to be.

In a digitized metaverse, where nothing ever really goes away, wading through all this material, not to mention figuring out how to use it, made me anxious. At times I felt like a pharaoh's assistant in ancient Egypt, the go-fer responsible for curating everything his boss wanted stowed in the pyramid before making his final journey to the underworld. You didn't want pharaoh reaching for something in the next life and finding it wasn't there!

I made a rough timeline of POTUS's presidency. The first inauguration was quite a party. But it was followed almost immediately by yet another animal-borne pandemic (chipmunks this time, the little bastards). Income for All was passed in the first hundred days, as was legalization of mind-altering drugs. The Venezuelan War came next — and, as wars so often do, made the second term a cakewalk.

POTUS dominated that next election cycle. Not that he didn't have problems, but as we know, he had a way of turning problems into opportunities — lemons into lemonade, as some poet said. Take the Fresh Water Rebellion (the beginning, btw, of Luscious's ascendancy). With fresh water becoming the new oil, we couldn't have people in the middle of the country hoarding what they had in the Great Lakes. Not with so many Americans fleeing the coasts because of pollution, wildfires and sea level rise. This became the basis of the Midwest Miracle, the development of vast tracts of wasteful farmland into vertiburbs, accompanied by the rise of indoor agriculture in the cities.

All this, however, was but a sideshow for the Great Rebranding. At the core of POTUS's second campaign was his call for a Constitutional Convention, followed by adoption (by acclamation, for all intents and purposes) of the Ground Rules, a governing document you didn't need a Supreme Court to understand.

After that, the third term was practically a *fait accompli*. Luscious became Vice President and honors like the Nobel Peace Prize, for POTUS's bold use of neutron diplomacy in the Middle East, began rolling in. Needless to say (but I'll say it), the last State of the Union speech deserves a special place in history, never mind the terrorist attack that took place outside the capitol that night.

The story we needed to tell required us to include all of this. But what about POTUS the man? Americans want to relate to their presidents. His/her/their lifestyle is, for most people, as important as any policy. The President exists in a vicarious culture where celebrity serves as both entertainment and edification. Let's call it the Elvis factor.

Our thoughts returned to Graceland, where Elvis was revered as a secular saint, Graceland serving as his shrine. As with Elvis, Americans reveled in the undisguised pleasure they thought they saw POTUS taking in being their alpha celebrity. Imagining what it might be like to be included in his circle of trust was the stuff their dreams were made of. Given our history together, this was a side of POTUS I felt uniquely qualified to explore. And when I thought about the part of POTUS's life people probably fantasized about with the greatest intensity, I thought of the women. The women most of all.

Which brings me to Del Capeheart. Now, I am not a racist. I mean I *am* — isn't everybody? — but I do my best to hide it. I have my share of built-in prejudices and I try to keep them in check so as not to get embroiled in the sorts of interpersonal dramas that can suck the oxygen out of a room. Live and let live, right? Whatever.

Without even meeting Del Capeheart, I was intimidated by him. He had published a best-selling book about presidential assassinations, been nominated for a Pulitzer and had a hit podcast. I realize that publishing books isn't a big deal but they remain totems, even if they're only used for interior decoration. Billy was susceptible to this sort of hoo-hah; he brought Del on board though the likelihood of Billy having read a presidential history were slim to none.

His interest in Del was amorous. They met at one of the inaugural balls following POTUS's second election. The chemistry of human attraction, so often a mystery, in this case was pretty blunt. Del flattered Billy, told him he admired his haircut. Champagne cocktails were chased by rounds of bourbon and branch water as Del held forth about the two Johnsons, Andrew and Lyndon. Billy was smitten.

Did I mention Del Capeheart was Black? He was also gay. More than that, he was 6'8" and built like a pro basketball player (a stereotype, I know, I know). Roughly ten inches taller than the average American man, he ducked when entering elevators, tilted like the leaning tower of Pisa while making small talk at receptions and cocktail parties. He wore his hair, which was polar bear white, brushed upward so that he always looked as if he'd been barbered by a wind machine. His eyes were a watery blue, his skin the same color as espresso.

I'd grown up being bullied by Black boys in my hometown of Hammond, Indiana. As one of the few White kids in my class, I tried to make myself invisible. Avoided the restroom throughout my entire freshman year in high school for fear of being cornered by someone like Del. God only knows what holding it day after day did to me. Perhaps this semi-buried memory accounts for why I put off our first meeting as long as I did.

Del's style was what the old hands used to call mandarin. He projected cosmopolitan flair and street cred, a wickedly glamorous combination suggesting depths of experience beyond the reach of most of us so-called knowledge workers. The man sounded smart even when what he said was obvious — like how presidents appear to age at an accelerated rate, or that most Americans are better off not voting.

The purpose of our meeting was for me to share my idea about the Exbots, lifelike animatronic simulations of POTUS's ex-wives. This was a brainstorm as far as I was concerned. I remembered how aroused POTUS and Juniper, his wife at the time, were by the lovemaking movie stars during their walk through at the Center for Performance Art and Public Spectacle. It occurred to me that having the President's ex-wives (all five!) cruising the library's galleries, greeting and interacting with guests, could provide us with an incredible array of storytelling possibilities. All the women would be represented as they were at the height of their respective erotic powers. And since POTUS, like Thomas Jefferson, was not only a singleton when he entered office, but remained a bachelor throughout his tenure, there was no current First Lady to upstage or insult.

Needless to say, permissions and, in some cases, rights, would have to be solicited and negotiated with each ex or her estate, as in (Billy's mother) Harley's case. Migraine-inducing questions regarding presentation, sexual politics and family values would have to be addressed. Naturally, I spoke with Luscious about my idea; she loved it. She thought the women (including her mother, Giselle) represented what she called "the state of the art, genderwise. Like *Charlie's Angels*!"

"*Charlie's Angels?*"

Luscious counted on her bejeweled fingers: "One's a former supermodel and the best chef in Portugal; one was a racecar driver; one is a spiritual guru — and then there's my mom. She's no slouch. Billy's mom killed herself, but she always seemed nice."

"Will POTUS approve?"

"When he realizes all these women are going to look the way they did when he married them, he'll wonder why HE didn't think of this sooner!'"

Both of us laughed. We could still laugh in those days. "Who else needs to vet this," asked Luscious. "Does Billy know?"

"Not yet."

"He'll say you should talk to Del."

"I'm sure."

"Ugh," she mock-shuddered.

Del Capeheart's office, like mine, was in the Eisenhower building, the French Second Empire pile next door to the White House. After Ulysses Grant ordered it built, it was, for a time, the largest office building in the world. When we got there, its interior had been repeatedly gutted and reconfigured. Our offices surrounded an atrium that flooded the place with a twilight gloom. Open spaces with oases of white Barcelona style chairs evoked the technocratic collegiality portrayed in the early scenes of Kubrick's *2001: A Space Odyssey*.

My office was two floors above his, but I coveted Del Capeheart's view. He looked through treetops toward the National Mall, where the Washington Monument stood under the chronically cloudy sky like a damp rocket, ready for take-off.

I think it's fair to say resentments simmered on both our sides. I suspected Del Capeheart was a poacher, trying to infiltrate a target rich game preserve. He considered me a starfucker. That we were both right should have made things easier between us but hadn't yet. That's the trouble with Washington — you are conditioned to think of every interaction with another human as a zero-sum game.

Ordinarily I would have created a written prospectus for a project like the Exbots. Something on paper that described them and how I thought they enhanced our vision. Such a document typically served as a discussion starter. But I refrained from creating an Exbot prospectus. A leak was inevitable and I was afraid an idea this good wasn't ready to be batted around in public. So I kept the Exbots dancing in my head for a week, while practicing my pitch in front of the bathroom mirror.

Del Capeheart's eyes were unsettling. The day of our first meeting, in addition to their usual wet blue they were bloodshot, making them look like a fair approximation of Old Glory. He fixed me with them when I gave my spiel, glowering like Jimmy Cagney's furious psychopath in *White Heat*. "You can't be serious," he said when I was done.

"You don't like it?" This question sounded lame, even to myself.

"I know we've come a long way from Reagan and Clinton," Del Capeheart spun in his desk chair and glanced back at the gray obelisk through the window behind him, "from Washington, for that matter. I know Americans think the presidency is just another form of entertainment, like football or porn. But this idea seems superfluous to me. Besides: all these women predate his presidency."

My heart leaped up. Never bullshit a bullshitter, as one of my professors once told me in library school. I immediately sensed that Del Capeheart's objection was based less on academic principles than his not having thought of the Exbots himself. It was his mentioning football and porn. Associating the Exbots with our national pastimes meant he found them more potent than he was willing to admit. "I think they emphasize the role women have played in POTUS's worldview," I said, adding, a trifle gratuitously, "his *weltanschauung*."

"You don't have to tell me about *weltanschauung*." Del drummed impatiently on the polymer surface of his desk with those extraordinarily large hands of his. "I support the idea of creating a presidential library, or center, or whatever you're calling this. It lends continuity to the public perception of our highest office during this post-constitutional period. But this idea comes dangerously close to making this project an adult entertainment destination."

"Del," I called him Del, trying to be conciliatory, "I must not be doing a good job of expressing the multi-dimensionality of what we're trying to accomplish. We want to build a permanent bridge between this president and the people. A place where everyone can learn about how this amazing man shaped our history. We want this to be the fullest expression of POTUS possible, so people can learn from his example, better understand how we got here and, yes, be entertained. Entertainment is affirmation, Del. We want everyone, regardless of whether they've been lucky in love, the color of their skin, their faith or gender or mental capacity to feel good about themselves and their president."

Del Capeheart rubbed his eyes and sighed. "Portraying the president as a playboy rather than a statesman…"

"Why so binary, Del? Why so either/or? Surely you can agree that his sex appeal is a significant part of his story?"

"It's retrogressively heterosexual. This isn't James Bond we're talking about."

"It's *Charlie's Angels*!" I exclaimed, This meeting was going better than I'd expected; if Del wasn't on my side yet, I felt him budging.

He picked a pencil off his desk. The high school freshman in me flinched, fearing he might use it to launch a spit wad at my face. He smiled and broke it in two. Like tipping over the king in a game of chess. "Have you taken this idea to POTUS yet?"

"I wanted to talk with you about it first."

"What about the siblings?"

"Luscious is for it. Billy is intrigued. Look, Del, I want us all to be proud of this. It's the librarian in me."

Del mulled this last bit for a second. "You wrote your thesis on Krupskaya."

I froze. Never in my life had my library school thesis come up in conversation. I wondered what else Del Capeheart knew about me.

He continued, "Krupskaya wanted Soviet librarians to be guides, able to explain to their peasant public why certain writings were important. I suppose these ex-wives — Exbots — can serve the same purpose?"

I laughed — a little nervously, I admit. "I knew you'd see it!"

We stared at one another until I looked away. My eyes found an antique photograph on Del's credenza. It was an unsmiling portrait of a bearded man in three-quarter profile. He appeared earnest and stiff after the fashion of his time. Wishing to end our meeting, but not knowing how, I changed the subject. "Who is that?" I asked.

"It's James A. Garfield, twentieth president of the United States," said Del. "He served 199 days, from March 4, 1881 to September 19 — the second shortest run of any president. He was shot by Charles

Guiteau, a delusional office seeker. Died from infection; his doctors didn't know about sterilization. In trying to find the bullet, they poked and probed his wound with their bare hands."

I grimaced.

"He was a Republican from Ohio. Fought in the Civil War. Chester Arthur replaced him. Arthur was part of a Republican faction called the Stalwarts. Guiteau was also a Stalwart. He thought if he killed Garfield and made Arthur President, Arthur would make him ambassador to France."

"Did Garfield accomplish anything while he was President?"

Del shrugged. "He appointed someone Collector of the Port of New York. His main thing was being assassinated. Lincoln was the first; Garfield was second."

"What a claim to fame."

"I study imponderables, Mutz. There have been four presidential assassinations that we know of: first Lincoln, then Garfield; after that, McKinley and Kennedy. Each represents a sudden departure from the historical flow. You can say these events were actually part of that flow, but they altered its course in ways no one could anticipate."

"You say there have been four assassinations *that we know of?*"

"Some think Warren Harding was poisoned. They think his wife murdered him because he was cheating on her."

HOUR 8:
PRETZEL CITY, USA

Palace intrigue, where the vain and ambitious compete for favor and influence, was turned to a ludicrously high frequency under POTUS, with the needle almost always in the red. We liked to tell ourselves this was part of the great leader's style. That he played people off one another in order to unleash stores of creativity we didn't know we had. According to this narrative, he was prodding us to be, if not our best, then our most effective selves. There was some truth in this — I mean, look at me now: taking a nuclear aircraft carrier for a solo ride. By myself! Scared shitless, but nevertheless. Fortunately, the ocean is huge — big enough for all my fears. All my sorrows, too.

Winning Del Capeheart's grudging approval for the Exbots was like a bullpen session before making my pitch to POTUS — live and in person as they used to say in the analog days. POTUS and I met upstairs, in the Treaty Room. Jimmy Carter signed the Camp David Accords there and it's where George W. Bush announced the start of his war in Afghanistan on national television. Presidents, going back to Hoover, have decorated the Treaty Room to suit their whims, making it rather like a Presidential man cave. POTUS painted the walls citrine, after the gemstone associated with wealth and prosperity. He installed simscreens and a sensory deprivation tank.

Unlike Reagan, who prided himself on never removing his suit jacket during working hours, POTUS wore a fox-colored velour track suit for our face-to-face. He nibbled chilled mango cubes from a saucer while Henry Mancini's "Moon River" played somnolently through ambient speakers.

"Mancini," I said, appreciatively acknowledging the classic movie melody.

POTUS nodded. "You know what it's from, of course."

"*Breakfast at Tiffany's.*"

"It's like a lullabye. I hum it to myself at night if I can't get to sleep."

"Beats Halcion," I said, alluding to how Forty-One, George Bush, Sr., famously passed out on camera during a state dinner in Tokyo after mixing this name brand sleeping pill with too much saki. In another era, this embarrassing incident would have taken place in private. Been the stuff of insider gossip. Bush had the bad luck of being President as omnivorous multimedia documentation of everything, everywhere was taking hold. His jet-lagged gaffe became part of the all-time presidential blooper reel anyone with a smart phone can download for free. Democracy by other means, I guess.

"I just had a massage," POTUS told me, a shred of mango stuck between his teeth. "A little body work does wonders. I can't believe I skipped getting massages during my first term. Too busy! Or so I thought."

"That was your period of adjustment."

POTUS caught my inadvertent movie reference and smiled: "Jane Fonda and Jim Hutton, eh? 1962. I was still learning to align peoples' expectations with my needs. Some things they know better than to even ask for now. Makes for less conflict. Greater efficiency."

We both sat for a moment, chewing fibrous fruit. POTUS said: "I hear you've got an idea. For the library."

"I, I wanted to talk to you about it," I stammered. He had ears everywhere.

"All my exes, eh? Digitized?"

"Simulated. Looking as they did when you married them. I call them Exbots"

"Exbots! With the possible exception of Juniper and, maybe Ava, I doubt anyone would want to see what they look like now."

"They're all remarkable women."

"Harley's dead."

"Yes, well…"

"But I was crazy about all of them, damn it. Up to a point! With some men it's watches or sports cars. Most guys, if they could, would trade places with me. I wouldn't trade places with them."

It sounded like I'd hit a presidential sweet spot, so I tore into my pitch: "The Exbots will greet visitors to the library by talking about all the things to see and do. Each one will have something humorous — though complimentary — to say about you."

"Like a Dean Martin celebrity roast?"

I nodded. "Some fun fact. They will also provide wayfinding information."

"How will they be dressed?"

"We'll consult top Hollywood costume designers for period accuracy, request proposals and leave the final decisions up to you."

"Let's have Luscious be involved."

"Great idea."

POTUS speared another chunk of mango and popped it in his mouth. "Wilhelm told me about this. I think he was a little spooked. He didn't have the best relationship with his mother, so that may have something to do with it."

"What did you tell him?"

"I told him not to worry about it. It's not his life. Not his wives!"

"Do you think the other wives will have any issues with being objectified this way?"

"Objectified? A couple will turn it into a negotiation. You can count on that. Lawyers will be involved. We may have to revise a couple prenups. But this is immortality we're offering. And they're all going to look great, right?"

I nodded.

"Let's not forget I'm President of the United Goddamn States of America," POTUS winked forcefully at me.

Presidents are almost always married. It's a sign of stability and their capacity for commitment. First Ladies humanize these powerful men; they can also serve as secret weapons. As Clinton said of his wife Hillary, "You get two for one!" Jackie Kennedy lent a touch of class to an otherwise philandering husband. Betty Ford was Gerald's conscience. Could Barack Obama have won his second term without his brainy Michelle?

I believe POTUS making bachelorhood a hallmark of his presidency was intentional. As usual, he turned the tables. Having been married five times, he saw being single as a sort of reassuring renunciation, his counterintuitive way of settling down. "I don't think it's fair to the woman," he'd tell interviewers. Or, "With my schedule, are you kidding?" Or (and this one makes my skin crawl), "I have a daughter!"

Not that POTUS ever lost his appetite for sexual adventure. At times he behaved as if the erotic magnetism of his office was his favorite part of the job. Power, as Henry Kissinger once so gleefully remarked, is an aphrodisiac. For POTUS, the libidinal alchemy of being president amounted to a salacious smorgasbord with unlimited seconds. Spanish fly? Ground up rhino tusk? Such nostrums were nothing compared to the Electoral College.

Trysts were a regular feature of White House life. The Secret Service invented protocols and passwords enabling whomever POTUS fancied to unobtrusively arrive at 1600 Pennsylvania Ave, gain admittance and, most important, depart — whether later that night or, in special cases, the next morning.

The situation got complicated when POTUS took a shine to Britain's P.M., Olivier Austin Triumph. Though she made a valiant effort at seeming immune to his charms — keeping a professional distance in photo-ops, closeting herself with counterparts from France and Germany at their first G11 summit — the Prime Minister eventually succumbed.

They were in the Alps, at Davos, making the rounds with billionaires in goose down designer jackets. POTUS asked Austin Triumph to accompany him on a tour of a nearby hockey rink. That she agreed proves Henry Kissinger's point about power, I suppose. The two of them were photographed riding a Zamboni across a plain of milky ice before repairing for fondue at a restaurant POTUS reserved for an exclusive dinner.

A flurry of encrypted, witching hour phone calls followed. There was a state visit to London for trade talks concerning pharmaceuticals and soybeans. The P.M. flew to Washington and stayed in the White

House suite where Churchill had a heart attack after a drinking bout with Franklin Roosevelt. She and POTUS cruised the Potomac on the presidential yacht, culminating in what the British tabloids called the Night of the Soft Landing. When Luscious asked him about what happened, POTUS told her, "FDR had Churchill in the White House. I've had Olivier."

Rim shot!

Neither party harbored any illusions about a future together. For one thing, Austin Triumph was married — not a particularly romantic union, but a fully adult partnership, based on tolerant pragmatism and shared investments. For a time, her liaison with POTUS provided both with a PIB, or Public Interest Bump. Americans took pride in their seemingly ageless leader's mojo, while Brits celebrated their P.M.'s having bedazzled the Most Powerful Man in the World. Austin Triumph was a vivacious 48; when a scrum of photographers caught her exiting 10 Downing St. with POTUS by her side, she wore a barely contained look of morning after mischief. This, I have to say, was the moment when we found that celebrity made the vicarious and the real one and the same as far as the public were concerned. Veronica Tu and I started making plans for a display we called "The Special Relationship."

POTUS's eschewing a First Lady made it easier for me to rally the participation of his exes. The lack of a Queen Bee gave them all a cache not otherwise available. Once I convinced them a) our invitation was not a trick that b) would in any way compromise the lucrative terms of their respective NDAs, nor was it c) a demented attempt by POTUS to rekindle old flames, they, to a woman, expressed their willingness to become virtual parts of history.

They didn't come cheap. We could have added another wing for the sum it cost to buy the rights to their 3D avatars. POTUS didn't seem to mind. The only time he balked (slightly) was when Luscious's mother, Giselle, wondered if, perhaps, as progenitor of *el jefe's* third term Vice President and likely successor, she was owed some added form of compensation. Arranging a private Virgin/NASA orbital excursion around the Moon for her and a select group of friends did the trick.

POTUS's libido appeared to reach a certain quietus early in his third term. "I look but don't touch," he told me in an unguarded moment, as we watched a lithe young woman carrying a placard with "What Are People For?" scrawled in black, walking in desultory circles with a group of sanctioned protestors in Lafayette Park. "It's a relief, Duke."

He was chrono eighty-five. Not that he looked it. Age Enablement made his face smooth as a teardrop. Blood renewal and selected organ replacements made it possible for him to cheat the clock in ways most citizens with their health maintenance packages and prescription attitude adjusters could only imagine. But as I can attest, Age Enablement and cultural momentum travel on dizzyingly different tracks. Deep down, POTUS could not change his being a twentieth century guy. He came of age when American cool, muscle cars and miniskirts, "sock it to me" and napalm were all the rage. I thought I detected a trace of nostalgic ennui creeping into his apex predator's forward-driving sensibility.

I wasn't that surprised when he chose not to make a personal visit to a hot zone in the Chicago exurbs, asking Vice President Luscious to go in his stead. An armed militia was blocking the old Interstate highway outside Rockford, demanding tolls and preventing convoys of water tankers from Lakes Superior and Michigan from reaching destinations in the increasingly arid and overpopulated Plains Region. This sort of thing was becoming more common in the country's former bread basket. Climate refugees from both coasts were making lifestyle demands and consuming more and more local resources. POTUS tried to diffuse tensions with a charm offensive, but the locals were having none of it. Their demands for a moratorium on fresh water mining and migration quotas only made him weary and exasperated.

"What do they expect me to do? Grow another Great Lake?"

Though his polling in the Plains had always been robust, he avoided going there if he could. He disliked the accommodations ("there's no place worth staying west of Chicago"), the food (in spite of his weakness for pork tenderloin sandwiches) and the people, whom I heard him once refer to as "hairy."

"Luscious," he said, "you go. And Duke, you go with her."

I was taken aback. This sort of trouble-shooting was way out of my line. "It'll be good for you to get your mind off my exes, right? See the USA in your Chevrolet — didn't Dinah Washington sing that?"

"Dinah Shore," I muttered. "It was Dinah Shore."

"I think it's good if the country sees Luscious stepping up. She'll be in this seat before long. Pack plenty of Kevlar, darling. Holler if you need anything."

Luscious, I could see, was thrilled. She was already toting up the size and throw weight of the strike force she wanted to command. "Thank you, Daddy, I mean, Mr. President," she batted her considerable eyelashes over the half-glasses she used to accentuate her seriousness.

POTUS sighed, turning from Luscious to me. "Don't you wish you had a HERbot?"

We cargo-jetted into Freeport, Illinois, a one-time rural crossroads about thirty miles west of Rockford, known as Pretzel City USA. Coastal refugees had grown Pretzel City's population to almost half a million; a cluster of highrise towers spiked upwards from what used to be farmland like nails through a sun-parched board.

Luscious was fitted out in designer battle gear: wraparound mirror shades, patent leather combat boots and a green beret with the Vice Presidential seal embroidered on the front. Her sidearm was holstered at her waist. Looking back, I must have been a disappointment to her — unarmed and dressed in a battlefield casual ensemble, topped by a helmet that fit me like a spinning salad bowl. A platoon consisting of two squads, or twenty combat infantrymen, accompanied us.

Downtown Freeport looked and felt like all the other exurbs sprouting in the middle of the country. Floods, fires, unaffordable housing and stratospheric taxes had been driving people toward the country's midsection, chasing the latest version of the American Dream, for at least two decades. Brand name restaurants, logistics centers and monster casinos blossomed where strip malls with tattoo parlors, nail salons and consignment shops used to be. You saw the same commercial facades and design flourishes in Freeport as in Emporia, Kansas, Mason City, Iowa or Baraboo, Wisconsin. Wherever you went, you were always there — we called it the Midwestern Miracle.

Freeport's Security Manager, a woman wearing plastic safety glasses named Gretchen, briefed us. She was built like a fireplug and spoke in brief, declarative sentences, occasionally punctuated by little, adenoidal barks. She told us about the militia blocking the Interstate.

"They call themselves the FarmerZ, with a capital 'Z' (bark). They pack fire team caliber automatic weapons and at least one shoulder mounted rocket launcher. All of 'em carry small arms."

Luscious stood with arms akimbo, legs spread and her feet firmly planted. "What are their demands?"

"They want to stop Great Lakes water leaving Great Lakes states. 'HellnoH2O' is their bumper sticker."

"How do I talk with them?"

I was impressed by how her uniform seemingly imparted Luscious with a focus I had not seen before. Since we were accompanied by a media entourage outnumbering the soldiers in our party by a factor of five, she was intent on making herself the star of this show.

"We've established Face-to-Face," said Gretchen.

"Who's the leader?"

"Levi Winslow. He's ex-Army. Former security guard. Processed pork at a local plant until they automated that. Rides a dirt bike and lives at the old Blackhawk Motel on Highway 14."

"Married?"

"Divorced. Owes child support (bark)."

During the twentieth century's Great Depression, armed farmers in Iowa fought foreclosures and unfair prices by closing roads to distribution centers like Council Bluffs and Sioux City. It was an agricultural strike; the farmers called it a "Holiday." Unlike those farmers, Winslow and his gang were better armed than the local paramilitaries sent to roust them. Childhoods spent holed up in their bedrooms, practicing for war with video games, made them an equal match for local government enforcers.

Some citizens had yet to reconcile the freedom they'd been given by Income for All with the abolition of social services — the Safety Net, as it was called in the pre-time. It's possible this was a design flaw in POTUS's plan, a psycho-social glitch overlooked by the policy wonks. But POTUS was an optimist. He expected more from people than they expected from themselves.

Midwestern rebels like the FarmerZ also wanted sovereignty over state properties, such as roads and bridges. At first, POTUS tried to buy these misfits off. That's the real story behind the Freedom Fund grant program. Critics called it a reward for misdeeds. POTUS considered it a cost of doing business. A flying squad from the 82nd Airborne was deployed to quell an uprising outside Lincoln, Nebraska. Then an armored brigade went to Indianapolis after armed insurgents attempted to turn the Motor Speedway, including its fabled racetrack, 18-hole golf course and the infamous "Snake Pit" into a "Peoples Republic." There were casualties in both incidents, though exact numbers are still classified.

Levi Winslow turned out to be a half-smart manchild. Resentment born of deep but narrow life experience made him reckless — something, I'm afraid, he confused with courage. Like so many retro Americans, he could talk for hours about what was wrong with the country. Ask him how to fix it and he was stumped. Before their meeting, Luscious conferred with POTUS, who made it clear that shipping Great Lakes water to other parts of the country was nonnegotiable. Deals had been done, an inter-regional treaty among several states signed. Moving fresh water was crucial to POTUS's plan for reconfiguring the still viable parts of the lower forty-eight states. Perhaps Winslow and his boys would accept a nominal percentage derived from a carrying fee?

As Luscious tried to explain this to him, Levi Winslow's

concrete-colored eyes gradually glazed over. He rocked back and forth on his campstool as if trying to stay awake. He was not bad looking. Unkempt, yes. I doubt he'd trimmed his hair or beard since the last pandemic. But he was in shape; looked good in the deer hunter camo garb that was *de rigueur* in these parts. A drugstore pair of aviator sunglasses were propped on the crown of his trucker's cap, as if they were goggles. When Luscious finished delivering her father's message, Winslow hugged himself and stared at the dirt beneath his boots.

"You don't get it," he said. "And with all due respect, the President don't get it."

Luscious: "I'm sorry?"

"This is Illinois." In stating the obvious, Winslow sounded a little too much like a high school smart aleck. He was, however, able to muster something like eloquence before he was done. "We're a Great Lakes state. Lake Michigan, Lake Superior — they make this part of the country like the Rocky Mountains make the western states. Cutting off the tops of those mountains was a big mistake. If you want to save this part of the country, don't truck the water out of here. It's ours. We need it. We shouldn't be penalized for having the good fortune to have grown up near the what everybody calls the new oil."

"The president understands your concerns," said Luscious. "He wants you to share in the bounty the Great Lakes provides and hopes you can see the opportunity awaiting all of us here."

Winslow shook his head. "I get that bounty every time I turn on my tap. It makes Illinois one of the best places to live in what's left of this country. Enhances my property value."

"That won't change," said Luscious, stiffening.

"Not so long as we keep it. You know, ma'am, sometimes I think we ought to just secede and take our water with us."

Luscious removed her sunglasses with cool deliberation. Her eyes were dilated, round and black as saucers — I wondered what she was taking. The economy of her gesture reminded me of Steve McQueen's laconic performance as the police detective in the car chase movie

Bullitt. She didn't blink. Her voice was uncharacteristically flat. "The president has instructed me to tell you that you have until midnight tonight to clear the Interstate for safe passage. Doing this will be considered an act of good faith, enabling us to engage in talks with you regarding just compensation. However, if you do not remove the blockade by midnight tonight, you will leave the government no choice but to intervene with the full force of law."

Winslow stood. I thought he looked a little confused. He covered his mouth with one hand and stifled a nervous yawn — his nails, I saw, were caked with grime. "All right, ma'am," he said. "I'm sorry."

"Don't be sorry!" Letting her imperious mask slip ever so slightly, Luscious awkwardly touched Winslow's arm with the tip of her ring finger. My heart melted. Winslow shivered. But that was all there was to it.

The blockade was still in place at midnight. No word from Levi Winslow. Luscious conferred via Face-to-Face with POTUS, who sipped Martinelli's in the Situation Room, the Joint Chiefs hovering in the background. He instructed Luscious to strike at 3:30 in the morning.

Two four-man fire teams were ordered to take positions within striking distance of Winslow's encampment. Though heavily armed, the FarmerZ were raggedly deployed. When the attack commenced, it appeared the rebels were not prepared for the Russian-style intensity of the rocket and grenade assault they were subjected to, nor for the merciless raking they received from the team's penetrating automatic weapons. Levi Winslow was killed in the first few minutes. What was left of his band surrendered shortly thereafter.

Luscious was photographed in the dawn's early light, a plume of smoke from the ruined encampment billowing up behind her. We enlarged that image and mounted it outside the entrance to the library's Luscious Wing. Her mother Giselle's bot was deployed there, greeting people and preparing them for the story recorded on a continuous loop inside.

HOUR 9:
IT FLOATS

Veronica Tu used to tell me her job was easy. "I bring POTUS printouts of the design. He says 'make it bigger.' That's what I do."

Architectural renderings were spread flat on a conference table in my office and weighted down with whatever came to hand: a brass eagle's head, an antique Lincoln Memorial children's bank, an old copy of Daniel Blum's coffeetable book, *A Pictorial History of the Talkies*, with its countless reprints of publicity stills from Hollywood's Golden Age — an era when every contract player, from Randolph Scott to Sonny Tufts, sucked in their guts and posed for obligatory poolside portraits. I found leafing through it from time to time a stress reliever.

Apart from the fact the AI program Veronica was using favored hard edges and sharp corners in a way I found a little on the Brutalist side, the library was beginning to take shape as a five-pointed testament to the most consequential president of the 21st century. There was just one problem: the Atlantic Ocean was feasting on the land Billy had acquired for our site. Thanks to rising sea levels, Salty Shores, Billy's supposed real estate coup, was sinking.

It's not like we weren't warned. A NOAA study, completed back in the Obama Administration, predicted major coastal erosion along Florida's Atlantic shore. This was just one of a cascade of papers, reports and projections — ranging in tone from cautionary to hair-on-fire — climate scientists issued over a span of generations. Evidently the residents of Salty Shores took these prognostications more seriously than we did.

There's no denying we behaved at first like typical sun-struck snowbirds. Even as seawater puddled up between the feet of surveyors staking out the site's dimensions, our team plowed ahead, dreaming up concepts, models and ad copy. No one wanted to face the facts bubbling through the ground, i.e., that the ground was getting wetter by the month. I suppose we believed we were invulnerable, although I know some of us secretly hoped we could finish the damn thing before the real trouble started. I must admit that I expected to be dead by then — or dreaming my life away at some think tank.

Somebody had to break the bad news about the site to POTUS. I took no pride in delegating this job to Veronica. That said, the relief I felt in passing the buck was palpable; my blood pressure scans were the best they'd been in weeks. I attended the meeting though, along with Del Capeheart. Billy was supposed to be there but was conveniently out of the country, scouting properties in Croatia. As POTUS fumed and fulminated about his wayward son, human gullibility, karma, the governor of Florida, his son, icebergs, the Second Amendment (!), real estate, retirees, God, and his son again, I watched the flesh on Veronica's neck turn from blotchy red to pale gray. Her eyelids fluttered.

"What's the matter with *her*?" cried POTUS.

I began patting Veronica's hand. Del Capeheart held a glass of water to her lips. Little drops, like tears, slid down her chin and made fuzzy looking black spots on the synthetic surface of her orange tunic. "Look," I said, not knowing if anyone, POTUS or Veronica or even Del Capeheart, was listening, "we'll get on top of this. We'll find a solution."

Del's watery eyes widened.

"Well, Mutz," declared POTUS, "you damn well better. Fish or cut bait!"

Fish or cut bait. No one had ever said that to me; under the circumstances it didn't sound appetizing. "Yessir," I said. "That is what we'll do."

It so happened POTUS was scheduled to hold a rally in Hampton Roads, Virginia, that same week. Called the world's greatest natural harbor, Hampton Roads is also the epicenter of our global corporate-military network. Bases representing all the armed forces, accounting for almost a quarter of the nation's military personnel, are located there.

Depending on your mood, it is either one of the safest — or most dangerous — places on the planet. Colonial Williamsburg, the Rockefeller family's fantasia of Eighteenth Century America, is nearby, as is the resort town, Virginia Beach.

I remember the day as if it were a lucid dream. The rally took place on the flight deck of the U.S.S. Gerald R. Ford, a recently decommissioned aircraft carrier. The Ford was named for the 38th president and hapless Michigander who took over the presidency following Nixon's resignation in 1974. Photographed tripping and stumbling in various situations, Ford became a figure of fun, a national punchline. After pardoning Nixon (ending what Ford called a "national nightmare") and finishing the remainder of his disgraced predecessor's second term, Ford was defeated by the Born Again Southern moralist, Jimmy Carter.

I had never been on an aircraft carrier and was unprepared for its immensity. The ship felt like the *ne plus ultra* of human engineering, a vast manmade landscape of gray steel, circuitry and pipes. The U.S.S. Gerald R. Ford was a floating airport, able to carry more than 75 war planes. Almost the length of four football fields (Ford, it's worth remembering, was a gridiron star during his college days at Michigan), the carrier was nearly 250 feet high and contained no fewer than twenty-five decks.

The Ford was also the most expensive warship ever built. I heard it said the bean counters at OMB gave up trying to tally its actual cost after spending passed the $13 billion mark. It was meant to be state-of-the-art: nuclear powered, with an electromagnetic aircraft launch system, multi-function radar and deployable lasers. But like the president it was named after, the ship's gee-whiz technology kept suffering "performance issues." There were tests and retests, design changes. Years passed. By the time the Ford was finally seaworthy, technology once considered cutting edge was out of date.

POTUS was supposed to address an audience of Pentagon big shots, members of the Carrier Veterans Association (an aged alumni group) and a large contingent of Boy Scouts (Ford was also the only

President to have achieved the rank of Eagle Scout). His speech consisted of the usual serving of honey-baked ham: practiced reverence for America's past, belligerence concerning its present, and a full-throated cheer for great things yet to come. Seasoning the oratorical glaze was a topical array of professionally crafted one-liners, planted here and there like dried cloves by the President's team of gag writers. People generally leapt to their feet by the end of these shows — laughing and wiping their teary eyes, shaking their fists. We called this reaction "the Full POTUS."

As performer, POTUS reminded me of Frank Sinatra as he was recorded at the Sands in Las Vegas during a live performance in 1966. Like that version of Sinatra, POTUS was still in reasonably good form, capable in both high and low registers, with plenty of swagger. Audiences loved that swagger. You could see it in the way they carried themselves after one of our rallies. This was especially true of the men — they added that little hitch, almost like skipping, to their otherwise humdrum tramping.

Things got weird — for me, anyway — in the supposedly funny parts. POTUS took a childish delight in making people laugh. It was one of the ways he flexed his power muscle. And, like Sinatra, he was not above indulging in an antique bit of white minstrelsy, adopting the basso Kingfish voice from the old Amos and Andy routines, even letting loose, on occasion, with a google-eyed "Holy Mackerel!" Hardly anyone remembered the origins of this racially demeaning schtick. Or, if they did, they stopped caring about it because crowds found these vaudeville turns hilarious. As comedians like to say, POTUS killed.

Rows and rows of folding chairs were lined up on the Ford's flight deck. I was assigned a seat next to Del Capeheart. Both of us wore baseball caps we'd been handed, emblazoned with the ship's motto, "Integrity at the Helm." The caps' visors kept the rotisserie-grade afternoon sun from searing our faces and scalps.

"I've never been a ball cap guy," muttered Del, whose too small cap sat atop his head like a toy.

I hardly knew how to respond to what seemed an unsolicited confidence. "Me neither," I offered, trying to strike an empathetic note.

"Ever been on one of these?" Del's considerable head swiveled from side to side, taking in the scene.

This, I confessed, was my first time.

"Gerald Ford served on an aircraft carrier during the Second World War." said Del. "This boat's big as a shopping mall. Remember those?"

I nodded.

He grinned. "It was the place to see and be seen. Cops used to run us out of the mall where I lived."

I realized that sitting side-by-side like this, with me looking up into his remorseless face, Del Capeheart and I could be mistaken for a ventriloquist and his dummy. I turned my attention to the stage, where the Marine Band was preparing to play a medley of patriotic country and western songs. That's when the light switch in my head flipped ON.

"What are they going to do with the Gerald R. Ford after it's decommissioned?"

Del shrugged. "Sometimes they sail them out to some deep hole in the ocean and scuttle them. Down they go."

"Seems like a waste," I said. The Marine Band swung into its arrangement of Merle Haggard's "The Fightin' Side of Me." Was there anyone in America who did not know the words to this classic anthem? All of us — even Del Capeheart — sang along:

> *Let this song I'm singin' be a warnin'*
> *When you're runnin' down my country, man*
> *You're walkin' on the fightin' side of me...*

My light switch moment percolated over what turned out to be a sleepless weekend. Conceptual shrapnel started flying in my skull as soon as it hit the pillow — I couldn't help it. On Monday morning I called Luscious. She was scheduled to attend a prayer breakfast with elementary school teachers but when she heard the urgency in my voice, she agreed to see me instead. "I don't eat breakfast," she said, as if realizing this for the first time.

Before heading over to her residence at the Naval Observatory, a Gilded Age throwback to Benjamin Harrison's administration, I scanned a photo of the U.S.S. Gerald R. Ford, enlarging it and folding it over like the gatefold cover of a vinyl record album. Presentation meant everything to Luscious; words by themselves were rarely enough.

She met me by the putting green Dan Quayle installed in 1991, the year before he and George H.W. Bush were defeated by Bill Clinton and Al Gore. It was early enough so that the District's swampy humidity had yet to permeate every thread and fiber. Luscious sat beside a glass cocktail table, sipping what looked like a Mimosa from a crystal flute and nibbling a crust of melba toast. She wore sunglasses with oversized lenses that reminded me of Sophia Loren and greeted me with a pout. "I'm still glitched about Salty Shores," she said. "Daddy's beside himself. I don't think Billy's ever coming back from Croatia — he doesn't dare."

"Well," I said, "I have an idea that could fix everything. I wanted to run it by you first." Luscious looked incredulously over her glasses as I noisily pulled a wrought iron patio chair over flagstone pavers and opened my briefcase.

"How was the rally?" she asked. "I heard it was boffo. Did you have to sit next to creepy Del?"

I rolled my eyes to keep her from stepping on my big reveal. "Have a look at this," I said, producing the image of the U.S.S. Gerald R. Ford as if I was doing table magic.

Luscious pushed her glasses down to the tip of her nose. "What is it?"

Being that we were on the grounds of the U.S. Naval Observatory, I decided to ignore her question's irony quotient. "It's an aircraft carrier," I said. "The U.S.S. Gerald R. Ford. That's where the rally was. We were sitting," I tapped the image with my fingertip, "on the flight deck."

"It's humongous."

"That's right," I said. "Humongous enough to be a presidential library! The first *FLOATING* presidential library ever! Luscious, we can build a marina and anchor her off the coast at Salty Shores. There's plenty of room for all the exhibits and programming. We can even include a boutique hotel for tourists and special guests. Restaurants, shops, a cocktail lounge. We can probably add upscale condos for added revenue."

"Duke!" Luscious's mouth looked like a valentine to me.

"Del said they usually sink these things in the middle of the ocean when they're through with them," I plunged ahead. "We could buy it for a dollar!"

"Ahoy!"

Luscious jumped to her feet. She wore a form-fitting skirt and her knees, which were practically locked together, struck the bottom of the glass table, tipping her drink and splattering my new Cossack shirt. Did I care? Did I?

Billy eventually made his way back from Croatia. By then, of course, the All Clear had sounded. POTUS was jazzed by the prospect of putting his library on an aircraft carrier and, under the terms of the new constitution, it appeared he did, in fact, have the power to acquire the Gerald R. Ford for a dollar, "in furtherance of Homeland Unity and Pride."

The Rebranding, also known as the New Constitution, would become the centerpiece of our carrier exhibition plan. Veronica Tu designed a special pavilion under the Flight Deck to tell the story of how POTUS made America relevant again by freeing us from the antique bonds of our founding mission statement. The pavilion occupied space once used for the maintenance of fighter jets.

The country's founding documents had become like aging relatives; regarded with awe at first, followed by the eventual appearance of various infirmities. These were patched up through wishful attempts at pseudo literary and historical interpretation — "Originalism," for instance — the time-travelling notion that a twenty-first century scholar could read an eighteenth-century founder's mind. Like a beloved parent in the grip of dementia, the Constitution gradually degenerated into an aggravating encumbrance, rendering national progress moribund. Its having been written in a cursive hand no longer seemed quaint; it actually pissed people off.

Many talked about updating it through amendments. Political dysfunction kept them from doing the actual work. No one wanted to tinker for fear that partisan gamesmanship could make things even worse. So the country kept playing by national rules thought up by slaveholding aristocrats, dead buried for almost three hundred years.

POTUS sold his do-over as a rebranding exercise. "If the Washington Redskins could do it," he griped, "why can't I?" The skeleton key was the ancient document's Article V, also known as "Godel's Loophole." Named after a refugee mathematician and philosopher who came to our country to escape the Nazis, Godel discovered the loophole in Article V while cramming for his citizenship exam.

Article V deals with amending the Constitution. The loophole is a logician's trick, in that there is nothing in Article V to prevent a President with enough congressional backing from amending Article V itself, in order, say, to change the rules by which the Constitution can be amended or completely rewritten. Given the misfit grab bag of celebrity wannabes serving in Congress, it became possible for POTUS to singlehandedly reimagine the Constitution, providing the Executive Branch (himself) with the sort of command and control efficiency Chinese leaders had used to dominate markets from Kinshasa to La Paz.

The desirability of this wholesale do-over was never in doubt. The question was whether the unruly study hall our congress had become could get its act together and do the President's bidding. After extracting pledges from the leaders of the top three political parties, POTUS enlisted billionaires from Amazon, PharmaPlus and the NFL to help him win approval in state legislatures. This was accomplished in the first half of Term 2. "Now," as POTUS so famously put it, "we can kick China's *pigu*."

Relief at being held harmless for the Salty Shores debacle was no less visible on Billy's face than his Adriatic tan (accentuating the blonde highlights he'd added to his comb-over). Croatia was "Brilliant," he said. "Really old, but new!" Billy was part of a group of investors acquiring a spa that dated back to the salad days of the Austro-Hungarian Empire. "Goulash and schnitzel," he giggled. "Who knew?"

According to Billy, my aircraft carrier concept was, "a stroke of genius. You pulled my chestnuts out of the fire, Duke." In addition to turning Salty Shores' dangerously rising sea level into a kind of asset, what Billy liked most about the plan was its provision for a boutique hotel. "Did *you* come up with that?"

I just smiled at him.

"You clever cunt! I told Dad I want in on that and he's given his blessing. I've got a meeting next week with the Four Seasons Group. How about this? A sea salt Jacuzzi in every room. Magnesium. It's good for the skin."

I couldn't help but be curious about what Del Capeheart thought. I knew from Luscious that Billy and Del had dined together when Billy got back to town; in fact, Del picked Billy up at Dulles.

"You guys have more in common than you realize," said Billy. "You're both storytellers! Del's a historian and you're a…a librarian. As I see it, you're both working for the sake of, of…"

"Posterity?"

Billy nodded emphatically. "And for the Homeland. This way everyone will remember how we turned the country around. Made it possible to live again! I mean there's a whole generation coming up that will never have to be defined by some crummy job."

Billy sighed. "Just give 'em the fucking money! The welfare state depressed people." He wiped his forehead with a handkerchief.

"I hope Del's on board."

"I know he can seem a little mysterioso. He's like a cat," said Billy. "It's impossible to know what he's thinking. But he's smart, Duke. We've got a hell of a team! This is gonna be great!"

Veronica Tu needed consoling. Seeing her plans for neo-Graceland circle the drain left her crestfallen. But POTUS made it better. He draped his arm around her and gave her a Presidential squeeze. "You're not going anywhere," he murmured. "Now you've got a big old aircraft carrier to play with." Tears of gratitude pooled in her eyes.

For the first time, POTUS seemed genuinely energized by the project. Instead of waiting for us to bring him ideas to shoot down, he began coming up with things himself. For instance:

"Duke," his voice like pearl dust in my ear at 2 a.m. Another in a long line of insomniac phone calls: "I know how we should kick off the project — what are we calling it again?"

"The POTUS Center?"

"I think we better revisit that. It's a ship. It floats, right?"

"Right,."

"Well, I know how we should kick the whole thing off. Drum up interest and anticipation before the opening."

"Yessir."

"I should be at the helm. On the bridge when we sail her into her parking space. I'll be up there waving, giving commands, as we ease that baby in. Perhaps we can come up with some kind of special uniform. Nothing too gaudy, not like what Chief Justice Rehnquist wore at Clinton's impeachment trial. You know, that graduation gown with the golden stripes? Something that says action. Like the boy's still got it."

This was the first time I'd heard POTUS allude to his advancing years. He prided himself on presenting a vigorous front: horseback riding, throwing out the first pitch at baseball games, atomizing a tank with our latest laser weapon. Americans reveled in staged exploits like these. And our strategically leaked reports of his amorous adventures only enhanced his Age-Enabled aura. That these adventures became fewer and farther between in the third term — were even fabricated now and then by the White House Press Office— was not perceived by insiders as a telltale sign of physical decline so much as the consequence of a demanding Executive Schedule.

Of course, as Del Capeheart reminded us, there was a storied history of creeping presidential debility. Woodrow Wilson's stroke. Franklin Roosevelt's wasting heart and lung disease. Reagan's Alzheimer's. In POTUS's case, a man who had once been full speed ahead, with little time for reflection or reminiscence, would suddenly, in the midst of a policy presentation on the virtues of robot pharmacists or urban farming, swerve into a digression on leading the victory march into Caracas after the Venezuelan War. "They wanted me in a bulletproof bubble," he chuckled. "Afraid of snipers in the skyscrapers. But I had a feeling, a sense of purpose. It was foggy. Pacheco weather, I think the Venezuelans call it. I said, 'Put me in a Cadillac, like Kennedy. I'd like to see some bastard make that shot again!'"

He was turning into an old duffer in spite of himself. If he was eating a hamburger for lunch, he insisted that everyone eat hamburgers for lunch because, he said, *they were that good*. The West Wing was redolent with the smell of grilled onions.

Luscious confided she was concerned about him. It was the lack of focus he showed leading up to his last State of the Union address. In the past POTUS had provided his team of writers and marketing gurus with an outline of topics he wished to cover. They would work up a multi-media approach — POTUS was the first president to turn the State of the Union into a Sound + Light production, a bit of stagecraft we would employ to great effect on the aircraft carrier. He relished what he called his "shows" and spent weeks rehearsing his delivery, polishing his phrasing and landing punchlines. This time, though, he projected a nonchalance that made Luscious anxious. She wanted nothing untoward to complicate the plan for her succession.

"When he said he wanted to 'wing it' I thought he was joking. Now I'm not so sure," she told me. "He said, 'Let's have this one be unplugged.' Do you even know what that's supposed to mean?"

"He's thinking of MTV," I said, taking a beat to mentally retrieve this rusty scrap of pop trivia. "*Unplugged* was a show where aging rock musicians played their hits on acoustic instruments."

"Whatever," said Luscious. "I don't know if this is the time or place for him to get creative. He seems distracted."

I volunteered to talk with him, take his temperature. Luscious set it up. The meeting took place among the red plush seats in the East Wing movie theater. POTUS was sitting in the front row, sipping from a can of Diet Coke with a bamboo straw. He got up when I entered. His suit coat was unbuttoned with his tie hanging down, suggesting the pendulum on a grandfather clock. "Hey, Duke," he called across the rows of empty seats, "you want to see a movie? I thought we should see a movie."

Entertainment conglomerates regularly sent copies of their latest productions to the White House for the President's pleasure. But POTUS rarely made time for these, unless he wanted to impress a foreign dignitary, in which case he made sure there was not only an unreleased film but at least a couple of its stars to hang with. What he preferred watching on his own were Hollywood classics from MGM, Warner Brothers, Paramount and RKO. For these he maintained a direct line to the Librarian of Congress, who dutifully delivered restored, mint condition 35mm prints. A mutual love for old movies was our *lingua franca*.

"What are we watching?" I asked.

"*Northwest Passage* with Spencer Tracy."

Northwest Passage, released in 1940 and directed by King Vidor, is widely considered one of the most racist movies ever made in Hollywood, which is saying something. The portrayal of Indians (the film takes place during the French and Indian War) is as lurid as the bright green Technicolor buckskin outfits worn by the "Rangers," Tracy's band of frontier guerilla fighters.

"I'm in a history mood," said POTUS. "Spencer Tracy. So fucking stalwart. Remember your lines and don't bump into the furniture — what he said is a lesson for life."

"Words to live by," I agreed.

"Applies equally to presidents," said POTUS. "Spencer Tracy, Gary Cooper, Errol Flynn: critics said they played themselves. That was the point!"

"I wonder," I ventured, "how Gary Cooper would have approached something like your next State of the Union speech."

From the eager way he nodded and grinned, I could see POTUS had been mulling this. "Think about the Lou Gehrig speech in *Pride of the Yankees*," he said. "Cooper's voice echoing all over Yankee Stadium: 'Today I consider myself the luckiest man in the world.' I watched that on a Sony Betamax. Goes to show you: the best formats don't always win. VHS was marketed better. And guess what? Everybody bought VHS. So much for the experts! You could say the same about me. 'He's a showman, no principles' — *The New York Times*. 'Lacks experience' — *The Washington Post*. Well, here we are, closing out our third term. I'm Mr. VHS!"

"You could hear a pin drop during Gary Cooper's Lou Gehrig speech," I said, reaching for our conversation's steering wheel. "About the State of the Union, sir…"

POTUS was ahead of me: "Luscious is concerned, I know. She's afraid I'm not taking it seriously because I'm thinking of doing something different. Well, she has nothing to worry about. I want my Gary Cooper moment, that's all. I wish Luscious watched better movies."

"She needs a guide."

A deliberately encouraging smile brightened POTUS's face. "Like you, for instance." This was not meant to be a question.

"OK," I said, unaware of what he had in mind.

"Luscious likes you, Duke. I've seen it. I think she needs you."

"Oh," I sputtered, "I think Luscious can take care of herself."

"She's next in line. It's been one thing for me to be President — Bachelor Father of his country, you might say. But I'm not sure America's ready for an unattached female. People are funny that way."

We let this thought rest between us like a warm croissant. Then

POTUS winked — just like he did with Veronica Tu. "Let's go to the movies." He clapped his hands. The MGM lion roared; we heard the sounds of fifes and drums and the stirring swell of Herbert Stothart's orchestral score. There was Spencer Tracy, not the elder portrayed in *Father of the Bride* or *Adam's Rib*, but young, eyes ablaze under a rowdy shock of chestnut hair. His men paddled across big sea waters, suffered privation in the wilderness and slaughtered Indians with muskets, bayonets and tomahawks. If at times they looked exhausted; that didn't stop them. They marched, proud but modest, into a Technicolor sunset.

I found it difficult to get into the film at first. The thrust of POTUS's remarks regarding Luscious and myself was unsettling. By the second reel, though, *Northwest Passage*'s self-righteous savagery took over, just as it surely had in 1940. A White House valet brought us popcorn. POTUS offered me a chewy red Twizzler from a Presidential pack. When the lights came up, we both blinked and stood, a little unsteady from our respective blood pressure meds. We said our farewells and I was heading toward the exit when POTUS called after me: "Duke!"

I turned. The President, standing up, in front of the silver screen, looked pixelated. "Mondo POTUS!"

"Sir?"

"Mondo POTUS! The new name for our thing! Our library ship: Mondo POTUS!"

"Mondo POTUS," I said, sounding like Audrey Hepburn as Eliza Doolittle, practicing her vowels in *My Fair Lady*.

"That's right!" POTUS shook his fists like a boxing champ, "I think we've got it!"

HOUR 10:
ATTACKED!

As usual, the holograms of Senators and Representatives were installed in their assigned places in the House chamber prior to POTUS's last State of the Union address. Outside, on Pennsylvania Avenue, the route from the White House to the Capitol was scrubbed of every living thing. Not even pigeons were allowed. Sharp shooters took positions on the rooftops of buildings facing the boulevard, police in full battle dress formed a *cordon sanitaire* extending for blocks in all directions. It was as if a neutron bomb, a weapon sparing the built environment while killing every living thing — the kind of bomb POTUS used in the Middle East to Nobel Peace Prize-winning effect — had been detonated at the corner of Pennsylvania Ave and 12th Street.

Over the years, POTUS turned the House of Representatives chamber into a high-end production facility for the purpose of making his annual State of the Union speech a must-see event, like the Super Bowl. His Veep, in this case Luscious, acted as emcee, calling out to the country that…Live! From Washington, D.C., the State of the Union with…POTUS! was about to begin. My job involved recruiting the "very special guests." Celebrities were called upon to laugh or weep or crack wise about various Administration Highlights. Some participated in a brief skit or blackout routine illustrating, via self-deprecating humor, the President's steadfast determination to make sure every American received their weekly cash installment, equal access to attitude enhancers and simulated experiences.

A lot was riding on this final address. Although early polling indicated Luscious was the consensus candidate to replace him, POTUS wanted to guarantee a seamless transition. The dust-up with the freshwater rebels put him on edge. If the new constitution made voting more difficult, it didn't guarantee Luscious's succession. POTUS wanted his citizen militias, the Call Me Crazies, in every state to shame potential rivals into acquiescence. Hence his desire for a "Gary Cooper" moment. He didn't just want to make people cry, he wanted to stake a lasting claim for his daughter.

Production values were high as ever, but more subtle. This time POTUS had the House chamber transformed into a presidential cabaret, where storytelling gave way to intimate revelation. He later told me he was tempted to smoke a cigarette, use it as a prop the way Sinatra did, but decided this was too retrograde for his audience. He did, however, wear a tuxedo, a look no other President had ever attempted for an address of this type.

PrePOTUS, the State of the Union generally opened with the President being announced by the House Sergeant at Arms. Then he/she/they — the President, that is — entered from the back of the chamber, glad-handing members of Congress on the way down the center aisle to the rostrum, where remarks were delivered. In reimagining this stagecraft, POTUS borrowed heavily from some of the more successful opening numbers associated with old Oscar telecasts (the Billy Crystal years, in particular). For this final address, he made things simple, even austere. Instead of standing at the rostrum, he used a stool, placed in the well of the House chamber, illuminated by a single spotlight. A microphone and stand were close at hand with a glass of water on the side. We used six cameras. Camera #1 opened on POTUS already sitting there, one leg bent, his world-weary gaze directed toward the upper reaches of the empty gallery.

Maybe you're one of the millions who found themselves fighting back the tears when you first saw POTUS sitting there. The entire nation took a deep breath and held it until the President, facing the camera's convex eye, intoned those achingly familiar words: "My fellow Americans..."

He spoke of the journey he — and we! — had taken. The ups and downs, the smiles, the frowns. How — together — we had done away with unemployment by getting rid of jobs. Brought peace to the Western Hemisphere by waging "a war we knew we could win," and finally, made voting a personal choice, not a civic responsibility.

"We've seen our country rebrand itself," he said, referring to the new Constitution. POTUS spoke of how warming temperatures and sea level rise had created "a Midwestern Miracle" in the nation's heartland. And more: the legalization of drugs ("way overdue"), the nationalization of online schooling for every child ("because home is where you learn life lessons"), the conversion of national parks into Museums of Nature, available virtually through streaming services run by the Smithsonian. "Just because we're all alone in this life doesn't mean we have to be lonely," said POTUS, looking over his shoulder at Camera #4. "You know, these past twelve years have been a blessing for us all. Being here with you, for you. It's — wait a minute! Who's this?"

The pop songstress Purple Martin tip-toed into the light, standing shyly to the President's left. She wore a silver ball gown and carried an electric guitar, suggestively shaped like a rocket ship. Though she must have been fifty years younger than POTUS, you sensed a powerful attraction between the two. Her slightly abashed grin was fetching. Her eyes, enhanced by contact lenses, were blue as sapphires. "Mr. President," she whispered, approximating a curtsey.

"It's Purple Martin!" POTUS exclaimed, altering the mood for the audience at home. "Tell me darling, what's a nice girl like you doing in a big old dive like this?"

"Well," said Purple Martin as a mime's pair of white-gloved hands shoved a stool out of the darkness behind her, "I've come to sing you a song."

"Is this my lucky day, or what?" said POTUS, mugging for Camera #2.

"Would you like that?" Purple Martin needlessly asked, arranging herself atop her stool. A shaft of her long blonde hair momentarily obscured her face; POTUS reached over and gently swept it back. She giggled, "Thank you, Mr. President."

"That's a beautiful…guitar," noted POTUS, assessing his guest.

Purple Martin ran her finger across the amplified strings. They made a tubular curtain of sound that reverberated in the large hall. "I hear this is one of your favorites," she said. "It's called 'Moon River.'"

POTUS leaned back, obviously gobsmacked with pleasure, as Purple Martin played Henry Mancini's wistful melody. "Moon River," she sang, her waifish voice trembling like a glass of water in a modest earthquake, "wider than a mile. I'm crossing you in style one day…"

POTUS wiped away a tear. So did you, I bet. I doubt there was a dry eye from sea to shining sea.

Billy threw an after-party at the St. Regis, a stone's throw from the White House. Architecturally accented with red and gold, the old hotel twinkled like a Czarina's wedding cake. The highly polished surfaces of black Secret Service transport vehicles blockading the building reflected ambient light like infinity pools.

At least two hundred Administration insiders mingled in the Beaux Arts ballroom under the watchful eyes of security agents and Billy's handpicked squad of musclemen. The mood, in spite of an incongruously loud band, was bittersweet. While everyone agreed that POTUS's performance was aces, there was also that taste of melancholy you get when the final curtain comes down on a genre-defining act. "I grew up with him," said Veronica Tu, trying (unsuccessfully) to nurse a foggy fizz of gin, limoncello, CO_2 and nitrous oxide. "He's my el Presidente," she said in a cartoonishly high-pitched voice. "He always will be."

Luscious was supposed to make an appearance and, it was whispered, POTUS himself. Billy, dressed like his father in a tux, was ecstatic. He considered Luscious's election a *fait accompli*. "Finally," he said, "the country will see what a truly seamless transition of power looks like." There was talk (Billy said it several times) that he was first in line for the position of Secretary of Housing and Urban Development in a Luscious administration. "I'm positive she'll pick the best person for the job," he could barely keep from laughing.

Del Capeheart was more jovial than I was used to seeing him, geeked by the historical moment we were living through. "Reminds me of Clinton's State of the Union in '98," he shouted over the band playing country anthems into my Age Enabled ear.

I nodded my head, as if I knew what he was talking about. In '98 I was still working at CPAPS, cleaning up after senile beatniks.

"Monica Lewinsky!" Del hollered. "The semen-stained dress! Clinton humiliated, his marriage in shambles. Everybody wondering what's he gonna say? Will he apologize? Beg for mercy?" Del snagged a flute of Veuve Clicquot from a passing tray. "None of it! He sticks 'em with the first balanced budget in thirty fucking years!"

"Took balls," I said.

Del jumped from one presidency to another, "Tonight was Reaganesque," he cried. "Star power. What you see when a man owns the office."

"End of an era," I tried not to yell, but the band made conversing stupid.

"You'll miss him," bellowed Del.

"Not yet," I said hoarsely. "Not until the library's done."

Del raised his glass. There was a glint in his eye. "Keep the faith, baby," is what I think I heard him say. An old-time battlecry.

The State of the Union always makes me thirsty for some reason; I'd put away a couple of Jack and Cokes — used them to wash down a gummy of THC I'd chewed before the event. I was about to go and get another drink when a commotion outside the ballroom grabbed my attention. Coiffed heads turned. Bodies froze in their expensive outfits. It was like that scene in Bambi, when all the forest animals smell smoke.

Del, standing a full head above the crowd, was tracking Billy, who climbed gracelessly up, over the front edge of the bandstand, his bow tie ridiculously askew. The Emcee, a young Black man wearing a cardboard crown, solicitously handed Billy a microphone. "Is this on?" asked Billy, his voice caroming from one rococo corner of the ceiling to the next.

"I have just received some breaking news," he declared. "Luscious, my sister — the Vice President — has been attacked outside the capitol!"

The crowd gasped. "The President," Billy continued, "is safe. Security forces have been deployed. You — we, I mean — are to shelter in place here, in the hotel, until further notice. Until then, enjoy yourselves. I mean it!"

Pandemonium. Many guests made a beeline for the bar, where a ceiling mounted video screen was hastily tuned to 24-hour news. Others held smart phones in front of their faces. The more seasoned among us went directly to the front desk and booked rooms, knowing from experience with past bouts of urban violence that it would be too dangerous to chance District streets before daybreak.

I followed Del to where Billy was standing. He was in the middle of a scrum of his stony eyed enforcers, his back against a wall filigreed in gold. "They're on the other side of the capitol," he moaned, as Del reached in to straighten his off-kilter tie. "It was an ambush. If you go outside, you can hear the guns."

Most of us are able to ignore it, but brazen crime in the District is a fact of daily life. The same is true in cities across the country, where gunplay seems like a form of self-expression. If you're my age, you can remember the Twentieth Century, when certain neighborhoods were off limits — too dangerous to wander into, even if you were in a car. In that case, you locked the doors and rolled up the windows. These neighborhoods were tolerated and understood to be part of the larger urban ecosystem. They were ghettoes, with their own off-the-books economies. What happened in them rarely found its way to what was called Downtown. Downtown was protected by the three Cs: Culture, Commerce and Cops. It's different now.

Mayors pleaded with POTUS to crack down on the violence as urban centers started looking more and more deserted — like sets for the spaghetti westerns Sergio Leone used to make. But POTUS thought differently. MAD, the Cold War doctrine of Mutually Assured Destruction, inspired him. He reasoned that if we all had cause (guns) to be afraid of each other (more guns), we'd make each other safe (thanks to guns). Hence tax credits for gun purchases. Can anyone these days afford NOT to own at least one sidearm? I myself, never a marksman or hunter, possess two handguns: an Army standard issue 9mm Sig Sauer M17 (a welcome to the team gift for all POTUS Administration hires) as well as a vintage Walther PPK that Billy gave me for my birthday. The Walther was James Bond's sidearm of choice. I appreciated the movie reference, but found the gun a little on the heavy side.

I'm afraid the doomsters who predicted that gang-banging street crime and political terrorism would become indistinguishable got it right. In spite of the massive surveillance and draconian police powers afforded by the new Constitution, offenders (many of whom were still in middle school) were rarely convicted; there was little in the way of useful intelligence or, for that matter, deterrence.

I was in a quandary. I thought of my last meeting with POTUS, when we watched *Northwest Passage* in the White House movie theater. "She needs you," he said, meaning Luscious, his daughter, the woman he meant for me to marry. The St. Regis was just a few blocks from where the ambush was possibly still in progress; even on foot, I could be there in a matter of minutes. But then what? My M17 was buried in my sock drawer, locked in its cool titanium case. Not only had it never been fired in anger, it had never been fired. Perhaps the better (safer) course would be to stay at the hotel, close to Billy, Del Capeheart and the rest of our team.

I crossed the St. Regis lobby and pushed through the heavy glass doors onto Black Lives Matter Plaza. The night air was being pummeled by helicopters flying so close to the rooftops I could make out the helmeted heads of their pilots. Billy was right: I heard shots being fired in the middle distance.

In 1981, when I was just twelve-years-old, my mother took me to Washington, D.C. for the first time. We saw the iconic sights and, since our trip coincided with the Fourth of July, attended the fireworks display on the National Mall. Ronald Reagan was in the early days of his presidency; the systematic dismantling of the Federal Government as it had been understood by Presidents in both parties, from FDR through Jimmy Carter, was just beginning. The first president to openly mock the institution he was elected to lead, Reagan cracked wise that the most terrifying words in the English language were, "I'm from the government and I'm here to help." Great line. Wish I'd written it.

That was the summer after Iran released the U.S. Embassy hostages. Looking back, it's clear Reagan made the most of Jimmy Carter's inability to rescue those American prisoners. Del Capeheart claimed that just as Nixon and Kissinger scuttled Vietnam War negotiations for the sake of political advantage before being elected in '68, Reagan's people persuaded the Iranians to delay freeing the hostages until after the election in 1980, denying Carter a bump at the polls.

In any event, having the hostage cloud lifted put everyone in a good mood by the time summer rolled around. The Beach Boys played the National Mall for free and the aerial fireworks extravaganza was epic, bigger and brighter than the display celebrating the Bicentennial in 1976. Half a million people watched. Reagan may have been just a second lead at Warner Brothers, but he certainly knew how to put on a show.

Early that evening, my mother and I walked down to the Mall from the Farragut Metro Station. We saw then what I was seeing now — the famous buildings and monuments, arrayed panoramically from west to east, culminating with the capitol dome. But any similarity ended there. The scene in front of me as I slipped away from the St. Regis was dark. A general blackout had been imposed, only emergency lighting, reserved for storms and mass protests, was allowed. Anxious pedestrians scuttled like crabs for the nearest shadows as a clamorous streak of emergency vehicles from Homeland Security, Civil Defense and the Metro Police sped toward violence.

I kept thinking (almost hoping) someone — a visored cop in Kevlar, some paratrooper with an automatic weapon strapped across his chest — would stop me, wave me back to a brightly lit room full of people dressed in business formal, drinking imported champagne and exchanging glowcards and gossip. This never happened. Shawls of gun smoke floated over the sidewalks and through the bare branches of trees. As I made my way closer to the action, the sound of gunfire grew more sporadic.

The fighting took place around the arrowhead intersection of Louisiana and New Jersey Avenues; Columbus Circle and Union Station's façade of art deco arches were within view. Hence the name we've come to associate with this incident: the Battle of Union Station. By the time I arrived the shooting had stopped. Police and military vehicles were parked at crazy angles, as if they'd been spilled over the pavement, blocking streets and providing cover. Polyrhythmic warning flashers beat the night in colorful bursts as helicopters raked the scene with frozen columns of white light. Radio speakers squawked; armed troops yelled hysterically at one another.

Luscious's black Tesla Yakuza occupied the eye of this sensory storm. It was angled in the middle of the intersection, doors lolling open, its bulletproof shell heavily dented, tinted windows spider-webbed from incoming fire so powerful, accelerating to safety had been stalled. When the attack began, the lead and tail vehicles in Luscious's motorcade lurched to a stop; Secret Service agents swarmed out, fearing the Vice President's vehicle might be overrun. Two agents were killed instantly.

In the back of her car, Luscious was more furious than afraid. Armed with a light submachine gun she stored in a custom compartment under her seat, she threw her passenger door open and came out spraying bullets in all directions. Surviving members of her security detail spoke in awed tones of her impulsive heroism. One said he would never forget seeing the Vice President that night, firing away in her Elsie Chao gown.

It was a brief, if indelible, moment. Luscious made an irresistible target. A bullet (falsely attributed to friendly fire by conspiracy theorists), likely a ricochet according to forensics experts, struck a devastating blow to the immaculate cheekbone on the left side of her face. It knocked Luscious backwards, causing her to sit heavily on the pavement. A Secret Service agent shielded her until a rescue vehicle arrived. That agent's body lay in state in the Capitol rotunda for a day prior to burial in Arlington National Cemetery.

Plastic surgeons did their best. The first of a painstaking series of procedures took place later that night. Bone, soft tissue and nerve damage were addressed, particularly around the socket of Luscious' left eye. Swelling and blood loss were considerable.

Her face was wrapped like a mummy's when I finally saw her. Fortunately, the sight in her left eye was preserved. I could see it glinting through a slit in the bandages swaddling her head. POTUS asked me to be the one to inform her that her would-be assassins had all been dealt with. None, POTUS assured me, would stand trial, as none had survived. The only prisoner taken was found dead in his cell following a lengthy interrogation. "Tell her she's safe," said POTUS, who couldn't bring himself to go to the hospital in spite of Billy and Del Capeheart's entreaties.

Seeing Luscious there practically brought me to my knees. So many surgeries were required to put her face back together, the most beautiful woman I had ever seen looked like a late period Picasso. Her eyes appeared aimed in different directions. Her mouth tilted to one side. When she grew weary, you could tell that everything hurt. But anguished as seeing her this way made me feel, I couldn't bring myself to leave her side. Not because I thought my being there was essential to her recovery. The quality of her care was, as you would expect, nonpareil. What compelled me was more primal than that. POTUS had things backwards: *I* needed *her*. More than I had ever allowed myself to admit.

HOUR 11:
SUPPOSED TO BE INVISIBLE

Can anyone truly plumb the depths of a child's relationship with a parent? Some of us spend our adult lives in 5-D therapy without ever getting to the bottom of this original bond. POTUS's almost pathological aversion to visiting Luscious in the hospital begged the question: WTF?

Del Capeheart, our presidential historian, suggested it was a matter of security; that POTUS was advised (by whom?) that placing himself in the same room with his wounded second-in-command during what appeared to be an attempt to overthrow his dynastic ambitions constituted a gratuitous risk. Luscious, though, was more than a link in the chain of command. During POTUS's first two terms many Americans had come to think of her as the nation's surrogate First Lady. But never mind that. Ultimately, she was the President's one and only daughter. His absence from her bedside grew more conspicuous by the day.

It wasn't as if POTUS was oblivious to what happened. After receiving confirmation that security forces had treated the attackers with extreme prejudice, he locked himself in the Presidential Emergency Operations Center, the underground bunker beneath the White House's East Wing. The skeleton crew on duty there were ordered not to speak to or even look in his direction as he took a solitary seat at the head of the long, dimly lit conference table where George W. Bush planned his revenge for the September 11 terrorist attacks and Obama oversaw the killing of Osama Bin Laden. POTUS brooded, alternately sipping Martinelli's and Diet Coke, as reports from various news sources replayed the attack across multiple screens.

At first, I thought events that night had scared him. No one was totally immune to this feeling. All of us wanted to run and hide to some extent. Fight or flight. The temptation to scurry to our respective hidey holes was easily justifiable as the responsible thing to do. For the sake of the country.

But that wasn't what kept POTUS from going to Luscious during those first, shell-shocked days. In fact, POTUS made a point of showing how unfazed he was by taking a personal tour of the intersection where the fire fight took place — accompanied by the Joint Chiefs, the Chief Justice of the Supreme Court, the Attorney General and stars of Hollywood's *Patriot Muscle* film franchise. He even paused on the spot, marked on the pavement with luminous tape, where Luscious's car had been brought to a halt, lowering his head as if in prayer before giving what sounded like an acceptance speech:

"I want to thank everybody I see here today, as well as all the incredibly brave heroes who risked — and in some cases sacrificed — their lives to defend Our Nation's Capitol and Our Vice President from the gang of cowards that launched this attack during my annual State of the Union address. An address, by the way, that marked a truly historic moment in the history of State of the Union speeches. Thanks too to the stars of *Patriot Muscle* for taking time from their busy production schedule to come be with me. Art, I guess, really does imitate life. Right? Or is it the other way around?"

POTUS went on like this for another three minutes and change before saying, "The Vice President is a fighter! She's recovering beautifully and our thoughts and prayers are with her." As usual, he did not respond to questions.

It wasn't that he was too busy to make time to visit Luscious. POTUS was famous for ripping up his calendar when the spirit moved him. He did what he wanted, when he wanted. "It's good," he liked to say, doing a vaguely recognizable Mel Brooks imitation, "to be the Prez." It is possible I was the only one who got this allusion to a late, great clown of 1970's cinema.

I came to see that what kept POTUS away from Luscious was the same thing that drew me to her. The damage. The suffering. He couldn't bear it. Not just because she was flesh of his flesh, his only daughter, the little girl he carried. This wasn't *Fiddler on the Roof*. It was more like *Chinatown*. Let's not beat around the bush: he found his daughter sexually attractive. The desire was deep in some prehistoric part of his brain. He couldn't help it and he didn't want to try. As far as he was concerned, Luscious was the most beautiful of all the women in his life, which made her the most alluring and the most dangerous. Perfect, in other words. But that, cruelly, was over. Though Luscious lived, she was broken.

She understood this somehow. During those first few days in the hospital, in the occasional moments of clarity when the haze of pain parted enough to make comprehension possible, I could see her grief, not just for the loss of her looks but for the way what had happened to her revealed the miasmic swamp between she and her father.

Billy spoke for the family, telling the media that the President's coming to the hospital would be too disruptive. POTUS communicated instead via voicemail and texts I read to her. Finally, after five fraught days, he made his first visit, trailing an entourage, including Billy and Del Capeheart. They hung back as he stepped tentatively across the threshold of Luscious's hospital suite. I watched the color drain from his face when he saw her. "Well, baby," he said to her bandaged visage, "you look great." I pulled a chair over to the bedside for him. He remained standing. "You got everything you need?"

Luscious tried to nod her head. A bamboo drinking straw dangled from the slit where her mouth was supposed to be.

"I'm glad to see Duke's here. He always makes you happy, right?"

Stillness. POTUS turned to me with a managerial look in his eye that said: "She's all yours."

News of the attack on Luscious was received by world leaders with a mixture of public outrage and private angst. The incident's having taken place on the night of POTUS's farewell performance was regarded by many to be a worrying harbinger of global insurrections to come. What was supposed to be a smooth transition of power, father to daughter, was now in doubt. While friends and foes alike had become accustomed to American society's increasingly violent mood swings, the attempt on Luscious's life struck some as a particularly ominous escalation.

China vehemently condemned the perpetrators for their disrespect of authority, congratulated the Administration on the harshness of its rapid response and wished Luscious a speedy recovery. Russia sent a gold-plated wheelchair. The European Union collectively worried that violence was becoming our country's "primary form of discourse," and the Prime Minister of the United Kingdom stood in Parliament to affirm, once again, her country's "special relationship" with "its cousin across the sea." The next day, a spa package from Fortnum and Mason, including an ostrich plume robe designed by Ringo McCartney, with a selection of essential oils and teas, arrived by special courier.

Speculation about Luscious's political future went into overdrive. Would she run? Could she run? Some found the idea inconceivable under the circumstances; others believed her candidacy more important than ever. For them, the attack elevated Luscious beyond mere politics. It conferred an almost sacred aura, made her both a martyr and a survivor — a combination most politicians could only dream of attaining.

None of this mattered as far as I was concerned. During those first weeks of Luscious's recovery and rehab I took comfort in what I liked to think was our cocoon. The extent to which this cocoon inadvertently dovetailed with the connubial blueprint POTUS had concocted for my future, making me First Gentleman — was set aside. So too, for the time being, were my responsibilities regarding Mondo POTUS. Instead, my days and nights were consumed by getting up in the morning and calling for a Hummingbird to fly me up to Walter Reed in Bethesda, where I practiced my new vocation as Luscious's personal librarian.

I let myself be guided by Ranganathan's five laws of Library Science, specifically, Law #2: Every person his or her book. Luscious had never been much of a reader, but this did not deter me. I decided to use our time together to discover exactly what her book might be. Each morning I packed a bag with three or four of the old things, just as I had done back in my 20th century student days. After getting settled for the morning in the Vice President's suite, I proceeded to read aloud to Luscious. My first efforts overshot the mark. Jane Austen put us both to sleep. Ditto Dickens, Woolf and Elena Ferrante. Joan Didion sounded too brittle. Margaret Atwood too menacing. Joyce Carol Oates was too much.

I'm not sure what lead me to the Nancy Drew mysteries. The covers, I suppose. I was browsing — an activity that dates me, I know — in the last used bookstore near Dupont Circle. There I discovered a small trove — five titles — of the old Grosset and Dunlap series for precocious girls. They were an odd lot: *The Message in the Hollow Oak* (1935); *The Clue of the Tapping Heels* (1939); *The Mystery at the Ski Jump* (1952); *The Haunted Showboat* (1957); and *The Clue of the Whistling Bagpipes* (1964). These books were blessedly short, fast-moving and, in some cases, surprisingly spunky, with an appealing B-movie energy. They read like candy. From *The Message in the Hollow Oak*:

> *"Nancy," said the voice on the telephone, "you are wanted in New York City!"*
> *The eighteen-year-old girl detective looked a bit startled. Was this a joke? Or true?"*

When we came to the end of *The Clue of the Whistling Bagpipes*, a highland mystery involving disappearing sheep and a family heirloom gone missing, Luscious and I were mutually hooked. With 170 titles still to go, we resembled dope fiends picnicking in a poppy field.

For his part, having lulled public expectations with his visit, POTUS decided the best way to remain engaged with his daughter's recovery was to send her gifts. White House gofers were dispatched in search of treasure across the city and into the environs of northern Virginia and metro Maryland. Soon his daughter's suite was chock-a-block with stuff: antique prints of Civil War battles; a crash helmet autographed by Indy 500 racing legend A, J. Foyt; a Ming vase (genuine) containing a bouquet of purple iris (silk); a framed *Mr. Smith Goes to Washington* movie poster signed by Jimmy Stewart (certified). The crash helmet actually elicited a Luscious chuckle — this was encouraging.

POTUS's schedule, I have to say, was packed. Not only was it crucial for him to be out flying the flag following the State of the Union attack, a series of trips and events, intended to serve as a three-term victory lap, were already on his calendar. There were speeches at West Point, the Hollywood Bowl, Caesar's Palace and Yankee Stadium (where he did his version of Gary Cooper doing Lou Gehrig). Overseas trips took him to Riyadh, Beijing, Mumbai, and London, where an intimate dinner for 150 was hosted by his one-time paramour, the former Prime Minister, and what was left of the Royal Family.

The surprising thing — for me, at least — was that he never stopped thinking about Mondo POTUS. Text messages, cool and blue, zipped across my screens at all hours. Some were trifling ("make sure café carries Twizzlers") others profound ("MP [Mondo POTUS] should sail the Seven Seas, docking in many ports — a first!!!").

There was talk of a fourth term. Age Enablement made this conceivable. But what people failed to appreciate was that POTUS was a man who hated to repeat himself. "Remakes," he complained. "Who wants to see the same movie over and over?"

I don't know to what extent POTUS's future plans included Luscious. If he was concerned she might not be able to follow in his footsteps, or how the stress of campaigning might adversely affect her recuperation, he kept it, like so many things, to himself. That he underestimated her — that we all did — seems lethally undeniable now. It's strange to say, but her path to recovery was like a birthing. The ambush was her baptism by fire.

★ ★ ★

People, I have learned, consider relationships between older men and younger women with a mixture of revulsion and awe. The greater the age gap, the more certain people are that something exploitative or manipulative must be going on. What does she see in him, they wonder. What does he get from her? Money, prestige, ridiculous sex — there must be an ulterior motive, a forensic explanation. Images of old goats and gold diggers flicker in our deepest cranial recesses.

Yes, I was old enough to be Luscious's dad. How this affected the dynamics of our relationship, Age Enablement notwithstanding, remained stubbornly unexamined. Though our intimacies were many, we were never what's politely known as a couple. It didn't occur to me that this state of affairs would ever change. Indeed, when, out of the blue, POTUS suggested Luscious and I were an operable match, I came down with what southern belles used to call the vapors. I'd always appreciated Luscious's obvious charms, but decided for professional and personal reasons that it was better to consider her a pal. Striving for anything more between us — between me and anyone, for that matter — was a ghost I learned to stop chasing during high school days (our Hammond High motto: "Once a Wildcat, Always a Wildcat").

As noted, the bond between POTUS and his daughter was complicated, even dark. If fans of the First Family looked forward to numerous scenes of paternal consolation, hand holding and unconditional support during Luscious's convalescence, they were disappointed. He showered her with gifts, but continued to keep his distance. No one suspected an underlying rupture in this; the demands of his office outweighed even familial considerations and, if anything, demonstrated the President's undiminished capacity to focus on what pundits archaically called "the people's business." When the President began being seen in the company of a suitably gorgeous, rather giddy young woman, hardly anyone dared see this as an effect caused by Luscious's disfigurement.

POTUS met Nova Reynard in Nashville, Tennessee. He had flown there to celebrate the official opening of Magipower, the largest film production complex in the world. It marked the country's resurgence as a filmmaking hub just five years after Los Angeles was declared uninhabitable by the EPA, Department of Homeland Security and the National Endowment for the Arts. Billy, who tagged along to close a development deal on an assisted living community for aging country music performers, told me about it.

They were visiting the set of *Laissez-Faire*, the latest installment in the hit franchise about a corporate vice president with super powers. Nova Reynard was POTUS's tour guide, introducing him to the popular stars Race Basho and Ding Puck. She even helped polish his make-up while director Raven Ames prepared a scene featuring the President in a walk-on.

"Don't I get to kiss someone?" POTUS asked, in that half joking way of his that sometimes doubled as a command. "I should kiss someone!"

So Nova Reynard kissed him. Right there. Under the lights, in front of the cast and crew. Everybody clapped, laughing at the showbiz impetuosity of the moment.

"Now she's everywhere," said Billy.

Although few dared to say so in public, the resemblance between Nova and Luscious was too striking to miss. The saucer eyes. Those sapling legs. Nova looked somewhat younger — closer in age to Luscious during the first term — but this only served to accentuate the similarity, albeit in a way that seemed to turn back time. Not bad, if you were POTUS.

He began by sending for her with his private jet. A black, armored car was assigned to pick her up at the special gate reserved at Reagan National. As her stays grew longer, the pretenses for these commutes (she was variously called a consultant, a trainer, a personal chef) wore thin, as did her supposed use of the White House guest room where Churchill secretly suffered his heart attack. Occupying her time when POTUS was called away for presidential chores became a priority. Billy called me.

"He'd like you to take Nova to the Kennedy Center for the Bob Hope Prize. He'll be there, but he doesn't think it's time yet for them to be seen together."

The Kennedy Center Honors became the Bob Hope Prize when there were no longer enough artists of sufficient repute to cobble together a compelling multi-media event. A lifelong fan of the Road movies, as well as such cult classics from Hope's "Silent Majority" period as *I'll Take Sweden* and *Call Me Bwana*, POTUS created the Hope Prize to recognize the country's top entertainers who, as Hope had done, dedicated a large share of their time and talent to promoting the country's military. I tried to beg off, telling Billy I had a previous engagement — I was looking forward to starting Nancy Drew's *The Ringmaster's Secret* with Luscious.

"Why can't *you* take her?" I asked.

"I'm going with Del." I detected an impatient note in Billy's voice. "Look. I think the old man expects it. I mean, he would really appreciate it. Seriously." There was a pause. "And I told him you would do it."

Did Luscious understand what lay behind my breaking our cherished routine? Certainly. When it came to her father's machinations, explanations were redundant. *The Ringmaster*, as she so pithily put it, could wait until our reallife Ringmaster's wishes were served. And so Thursday night found me in the Kennedy Center's towering foyer of scarlet, crystal and gold, awaiting Nova Reynard and feeling not a little like Rod Steiger's amoral roue in *Doctor Zhivago*.

The girl knew how to make an entrance. She was wrapped in an animated fiber gown that made her body look like a sky upon which clouds blew round and round. Her hair was severely pulled back and her eyes shaded blue, like robin's eggs. Even though I was wearing a tux I felt underdressed beside her but that was fine — I was supposed to be invisible. I offered my hand as the crowd of preposterously coiffed bureaucrats, multi-platform celebrities and corporate monsters parted to let her pass.

"Mutz," I introduced myself. "Duke Mutz."

She laughed heartily. To my consternation, I suddenly saw in her what I guessed POTUS saw.

The program, honoring comedian, actor and retired late show host Stiv Rules was, as usual, fast-paced and polished. A cavalcade of Rules's colleagues and former co-stars trooped across the stage, including a retired Secretary of Defense and two five-star generals (whose timing in a sketch originally performed by Bob Hope and Bing Crosby in *Road to Utopia* was surprisingly effective). Rules, who spoke as if his mouth was full of marbles, having suffered multiple strokes, still managed to reprise a few of his famous zingers and even pulled off a doddering slapstick bit. In a poignant close, he said he was "honored to have helped everyone, from the foot soldier to the President of the United States, feel good about themselves." Nova, I noticed, threw a megawatt smile toward POTUS in his flag-draped box as he rose to his feet to lead the obligatory standing ovation.

There was time to kill before I was supposed to squire Nova back to the White House and we repaired to a lounge overlooking the Potomac for a drink. She ordered chilled saki; I asked for a double bourbon on the rocks. A momentary silence fell between us. This, I thought, is why people invented cigarettes. Nova broke the ice: "I don't know if he's really that funny, but Stiv certainly supported our troops…"

"I thought I saw you laughing," I said.

"The stroke makes him more compelling," Nova leaned toward me. "Who's that staring at us?"

I saw the Army's Chief of Chaplains, Major General Ralph Socket, giving us the eye over his reading glasses. He and a young Second Lieutenant were nursing Aperol spritzes.

"The Army's Bible beater," I muttered.

"God bless us every one! Washington really is a small town, isn't it?"

"A company town, yes."

"Were you in government before POTUS?"

"No. It was POTUS brought me here."

"From the beginning?"

"From the start."

"It must have been exciting."

I downed my bourbon and discovered I needed another. "It was terrifying," I said. "It felt like everyone was out to get us. The news media taking pot shots. Late night comedians making fun. Even Stiv Rules made jokes at our expense — until his sponsors disappeared. The first hundred days were a street fight. But POTUS prevailed."

"He bridged the generations," said Nova. "Before POTUS, every generation hated the one that came before. Yet every one that came before said it wanted to make things better for the one that came after. Sheesh!" She shook her head as if trying to clear it. "What a crazy way to think of progress."

"POTUS certainly simplified things," I said.

"Yes! I mean before POTUS everything in America was based on this exhausting idea of participation. That every citizen had a duty to wake up and fight for this or that or something else. Voting rights. Clean water. Fair pay. Social justice. Infrastructure. Education. As if people didn't have enough to do just to make a living. America was an alarm clock that never stopped ringing!"

I wondered where our waiter was.

"I loved it when POTUS said Americans should have the freedom NOT to vote. That was liberating. I mean, did you know women in Switzerland didn't have to vote until 1971? The rich know: voting doesn't matter."

"True," I said, trying to deflect a little of Nova's headlong energy. I was amazed POTUS could keep up with her. "POTUS has a gift."

"He's a sweetheart," she said.

"You don't find him…" I looked for a word other than old, "preoccupied?"

"Well, he's concerned about his daughter, I know that."

"Of course."

"He wants her to succeed him. He wants her to be healthy. That's another reason why I love him — I mean besides being my President and the most famous man in the world — he's such a good dad!"

HOUR 12:
PEOPLE ARE TROUBLE

Veronica Tu was fuming. "Did you know about this?" She was standing in my office doorway, brandishing a sheet of paper emblazoned with the presidential seal. Her eyes looked as red as her precisely painted lips. Such dialed-up intensity, first thing in the morning, was enough to make me forget Nova Reynard — for a little while.

I cringed. "What?"

"POTUS wants his aircraft carrier to be operable. He wants to sail it to other cities. Other countries! It's," she faltered, adjusted her volume, "it's a brilliant idea. But half the work I've done might be wasted. What if there's a storm at sea?"

"And the Exbots get seasick?"

She handed me the memo.

It appeared POTUS had awakened the morning after another witching hour brainstorm and, following his exhaustive daily ablutions, dictated the details on his smart phone. "Who all was copied on this?" I asked.

"You," said Veronica. "Me. Luscious and Billy. Del Capeheart."

I rubbed my eyes. "I thought he was kidding."

"You knew about this?"

"Barely." I sighed, trying to signal collegial commiseration. "He called me in the middle of the night. I thought he'd forget it the next morning. He usually does."

"Wow," Veronica could still be impressed by my insider status. Exasperation gave way to starstruck curiosity. She slid into the chair on the other side of my desk. "He calls you in the middle of the night?"

"It makes sleeping difficult sometimes."

She took a deep breath. "Has he mentioned me? Ever?"

"He's very enthused about Mondo POTUS. He's thinking about it more and more. He sees himself on the bridge, dressed like Charlton

Heston as Andrew Jackson at the battle of New Orleans."

Veronica looked at me as though I was Moses, back from the mountaintop. She nibbled thoughtfully on her lower lip, making a crimson stain across her upper incisors. "That's incredible, you know. It's visionary."

"What do you mean? I thought…" I was having trouble keeping up with her.

"What a symbol of Presidential exceptionalism! Docking in harbors around the world! I wasn't thinking big enough!"

"I can talk to him. I'd hate for all your hard work…"

Veronica stood. She wore a snug blue tunic with brass buttons and red piping that made her look like Michael Jackson. Very War of 1812. "Sometimes I need to remind myself: Girl, you have the greatest job ever!"

I used to feel that way. During the romp and stomp of the first campaign. The primaries and caucuses (whatever the hell those were): Iowa, New Hampshire, South Carolina, Nevada. The gray, airless atmosphere inside chartered jets; the scratchy upholstery on tour buses. The people. Millions and millions of people. Like ants, but with eyes.

In those days it was clear to almost everybody that the country didn't work. POTUS understood this before the supposed professionals. The professionals kept thinking what was needed was improvement or reform. The country had been good for them. Worked, more or less, as advertised. Obama, for example. A Black man for whom the system was practically tailormade. Given his self-discipline, intellectual curiosity and above average intelligence, the color of his skin was not an impediment but an accelerant for opening doors to the highest echelons of White Privilege. He played by the rules, albeit rules designed expressly to help somebody like him, and succeeded beyond all expectation. If his election seemed, at first, transformative, it was actually an affirmation of conservative values. That actual conservatives not only failed to celebrate this, but resented it was a bellwether for how dysfunctional the nation's politics had become.

By the time POTUS came along, this dysfunction was a given, part of the country's governing culture. That so many supposed experts claimed this mess was what the Founders intended when they created the separation of powers did nothing to bolster the ordinary citizen's confidence in where things were headed. Fortunes were made by businesses that never turned a profit. Productivity was decoupled from work. Wealth had nothing to do with value. Fame no longer meant accomplishment. Most Americans we met had been immersed in this soup for such a long time they took it for granted. Generations of Americans conditioned to think of advertising as art expected everything to be for sale.

Americans. We met them in those early days. In diners and bars, of course. And at the deserted shopping malls, weedy parking lots and abandoned multiplex movie theaters where their great grandparents had congregated in the analog days. Americans showed up for us in their ball caps and concert tour tee-shirts, tattoos, camouflage cargo pants and body armor. They wore their guns like fashion accessories; some cradled these weapons against their chests as if they were testy babies. They spoke of them as if they were pets.

Not being an outdoorsman, urban gangster or militia member, POTUS was a little unnerved by this gun lust at first. He learned not to let it throw him. Since he'd grown up watching Westerns, war movies and other tales of manly adventure, he knew guns doubled as a form of self- expression. During a rally at a bankrupt farm in Michigan he asked a fellow with muttonchops and a heavy set of man boobs if he'd lend the next President of the United States his modified Keltec RDB to "squeeze off a few rounds." It was like asking a racecar driver to take him for a spin. The fellow fixed POTUS with an incredulous stare —you can see it for yourself on YouTube — before realizing he wasn't being teased. The two of them walked like long lost brothers across a cornfield gone to dust before firing several bursts and startling a flock of crows.

★ ★ ★

We put it out there that POTUS was a risk taker. He arrived at a deserted street corner on the west side of Chicago — notorious at the time for its extravagant murder rate — pitched a tent and held revival-style rallies there for three days. Long enough, in other words, for the national media to start carrying them live.

POTUS rolled up his sleeves like Burt Lancaster in *Elmer Gantry*. Sweat made a dark streak down the back of his shirt. The atmosphere was carnivalesque. There were free hot dogs, cold beer, even cotton candy. Young Black men, inscrutable behind their sunglasses, stood like Easter Island statues, arms folded across their chests. POTUS told them they deserved their own police department, their own schools, their own banks. He made a show of hiring several as bodyguards.

It was all adrenaline all the time. A first campaign is like a start-up business. Your focus is bifurcated between the immediacy of the moment and where you need to be next week. You take a punch and land two. Eat on the fly. I loved road food (still dream about it): hamburgers and corned beef, pulled pork, pork tenderloin, brats and wieners, salami, melted cheese. My God! Greasy paper, greasy fingers. Everything washed down with Diet Coke — carbonated coffee! Our only plan was to be liked. Liked a lot. Owning the room in Kenosha, Riverside, Carbondale. We slept in snatches like saddle tramps; sleep deprivation made us sharper (or so we told ourselves), hyper-articulate, ready to pounce.

What did Mencken say? "Nobody ever went broke underestimating the intelligence of the American people," or words to that effect? We brought Mencken up to date. POTUS made people feel that being cynical was smart, tough, realistic. Some laughed at him, but he didn't mind if they thought he was funny; it meant they would come back for another helping.

POTUS knew how to win. That's what comes through about the first campaign. One pundit likened him to Sherman marching to the sea. Another compared him to Tom Brady driving for the endzone. A general and a quarterback: the ultimate playmaking American icons. POTUS presented himself as being able to score a touchdown in the middle of a battlefield.

After winning the first time, we learned governing had a different rhythm. Where campaigning was a four-alarm blaze, governing was a lowgrade fever. I leased a District apartment in the Dorchester, a blonde deco building on 16th St. across from Meridian Hill Park. JFK, I was told, slept there from time to time after World War II. I made a hasty job of decorating the place, tacking up some reproductions from the Phillips Collection. I liked Alex Katz's portrait of a patrician-looking woman called *Brisk Day II* because she exuded what I considered *savoir faire*. Modigliani's portrait of Elena Povolosky was an inside joke; I thought she bore a striking resemblance to Billy. And Thomas Hart Benton's *Moonlight on the Osage*, with its foreboding blues and sharp, upthrusting angles, rhymed somehow with how I was feeling about what I started calling my "career."

The commute to the Executive Office Building, where I had an office with my name on the door and a wall of built-in video screens was easy. I went to lunches in restaurants with white tablecloths. Took meetings. Made presentations. I settled into my new city, new life, like a leaf in a window well.

I really did feel like Veronica in those days. Eager. Thrilled to be at the center of things. Glad, above all, to have a job when millions were out of work and probably wondering why they'd ever been born. I was lucky and I knew it, which was hard in a way because when people asked me how I got my job (or career), I felt embarrassed. Saying all this happened to me because I accepted a free cocktail one night in Palm Beach, couldn't help anybody's life plan. That's luck: If the right person takes a liking to you, the rest takes care of itself. It's like the Christian notion of predestination: being picked in the womb by God to be one of the select who get to go to Heaven. Nothing you can plan or do really matters. That's not an American idea — we're taught to believe hard work pays off — but I've found it's the way things usually work.

I thought of Nova Reynard, the jolt she doubtless brought to POTUS's private life and the platform being so close to POTUS provided her. In any other place, their relationship would have seemed like something from a Southern Gothic potboiler. Not in Our Nation's Capital, where his power and her ambition looked made for each other.

And Luscious. How I wished we could run away together, far from the Peoples' Business. Someplace where I could simply read Nancy Drew mysteries to her and she could heal. There were times I thought the attempt on her life had a greater effect on me than her. While I wondered if the cost of leadership in a country as prone to violence and inchoate resentment as ours was worth it, Luscious, from her bed in Walter Reed, whispered her intention to come back, stronger, better, more determined than ever.

It was Luscious who thought of making her candidacy for President virtual. This came after her fifth plastic surgery, a procedure that made her complexion appear translucent, not unlike those plasticene street lamps they've installed for pedestrians in the tunnels beneath Las Vegas. She thought things through and concluded a virtual candidate would be accepted by voters, who might find he/she/they more attractive than the real thing.

"Everybody knows how crazy people can be," she told me. "Even Daddy has his moods," she rolled her one operable eye, making me think she was still a teenager at heart. God, I was smitten. "I think a virtual President makes sense," she continued. "You can feed it — me, us, I mean — all the information about any problem and we'll find a solution. We'll do what's right. Every time! That's not a bad slogan, is it?"

I nodded, impressed.

"And a virtual candidate," Luscious lowered her voice, "wouldn't have to worry about her looks."

"You're a goddess," I said. "An inspiration. Everybody knows what you've been through."

Luscious looked at me; the surgeries made it difficult to read the expression on her face. She appeared to be terminally bemused. "Make an Exbot of me. Make me appear as I was. Before…"

Sun Tzu, in his *Art of War*, could not have been more lucid. "I wish I'd thought of that," I said.

"But I'm glad you didn't," said Luscious. "You take me as I am. That's wonderful, Duke. But I can be better, and this is how. There's no reason the President needs to be a person. And since no one will ever truly replace Daddy…"

"Did you think of that?" POTUS beamed at me from behind the Resolute Desk when I mentioned running a virtual Luscious for President — I assumed that, like most things, he already knew about it. "Because that's perfect. Exactly what the country needs."

I'm embarrassed to say I did not immediately disabuse him of the notion that I deserved the credit he so quickly threw my way. "I'm glad you think so, sir." I still called him sir.

POTUS rocked back in his padded chair, extending his arms to either side, like the eagle on the Presidential seal. I imagined him with talons beneath that great desk, gripping a sheaf of olive branches on one side and a clutch of arrows on the other. Half man, half raptor — like one those chimerical hybrids in *The Island of Doctor Moreau*. "Let's face it, Duke," he said, "The job's too big for most people. We've turned everything else over to machines, why not the Presidency? In a strange way I think having a double makes Luscious more approachable."

"Yes?"

"People are trouble. You can trust a machine. Until it breaks down, of course. Then you replace it." He swiveled in his chair and coughed, "And there's the looks factor."

I felt my forehead tingle. "She will always look like her best self."

POTUS nodded vigorously. "People want to see what they expect to see. They want her put together. She does too! Nobody wants to see me raw in the morning. Ask Nova. I thought she'd scream the first time we woke up together."

"I'm sure she didn't scream, sir."

"No, as a matter of fact she did not." POTUS winked. Or maybe it was that pesky tic he sometimes got after too many Diet Cokes. "The point is, designing ourselves is what civilized people do."

"I think Luscious worries you might think she's lost her ch'i," I said, referring to the ancient Chinese principle of unimpeded life force. POTUS and Luscious shared a brief but intense craze for China's traditional healing arts following a White House performance by a troupe of kung fu fighters during the first term. For a while there, all of us were drinking green tea.

"Lost her *ch'i*? Not my girl. This isn't Wilhelm we're talking about. Sweet boy, don't get me wrong. Throws a hell of a party. But does anybody picture him jumping out of that car, guns blazing? And in heels?"

He was right, of course.

"Luscious is made of tougher stuff," POTUS continued. "It gets me sometimes how like her Nova can be. They both have that energy. I'm sure you've seen it."

"Nova has a great laugh," I nodded.

"She does!" POTUS leaned forward, his elbows making hoof-like indentations in the blotter on his desk. "I want to thank you, Duke, for sticking so close to Luscious during this shitstorm. Don't think I haven't noticed. As you know, I've always thought you two belonged together."

I could have asked why it was me and not him who stayed by Luscious's side as she clawed her way back to consciousness. Why it was me reading her Nancy Drew mysteries every night. Me who brought him her decision to run a virtual campaign. Here is what I said instead:

"I agree."

A little brat inside me relished the prospect of being the first to tell Del Capeheart about Luscious's virtual candidacy. The brat loves being an insider, having the scoop, the breaking news. I like the brat. He's entertaining. But the brat is just one of the competing voices in my head, which may account for why I've lived long enough to tell this story now. Much as I looked forward to seeing Del's reaction when I told him his scholarly view of Presidential continuity was about to become obsolete, I also needed him on my side.

"Do you play golf?" Del's baritone sounded remarkably upbeat. He was headed out to hit some balls on the practice range at Congressional in Bethesda. Congressional has a history among golfing presidents. Taft, Wilson, Coolidge, Hoover — they all helped found it in 1924. During World War II Congressional was used as a training ground for the OSS cloak and dagger boys. The place boasted a tennis club, grand ballroom, several swimming pools and eight different venues serving food and drink.

I met Del in the Founders Pub, a room John Ford might have conjured in one of his homoerotic Irish daydreams. The room gleamed with polished wood and comfy leather. Antique golf clubs, crossed like cavalry sabers, were mounted above the bar. Del dressed for the setting, wearing green puttees, a red polo shirt and an argyle sweater. I tried to look at ease in my corduroy Nehru jacket. Both of us ordered burgers. Del insisted the meal was on him.

"You're probably wondering how I afford this, since the entry fee's $150 grand and the wait's ten years. But like everything in this town, it's who you know."

Billy, I thought.

"Billy's been a big help," he said, reading my mind. "He knows I'm a golf nut. And it's helpful, on occasion, to be able to meet," he smiled, "like this. I must say that there are times when I'm afraid someone will ask me to carry his bag or shine his shoes, but I get a kick out of imagining Coolidge playing Hoover for lemonades. Calvin making Herbert tremble over a two-foot putt to see who buys."

I wondered where Del learned to play. "In a vacant lot the size of a city block. Philly. An old gas main exploded — Black neighborhood. People smelling it for days but no one checked it out. Took down all the old houses, killed a bunch of people. The city bulldozed everything and we kids claimed it. I found an old set of clubs in a dumpster. We laid out a little course. Instead of holes we had landmarks, like you had to hit the ball up to an old hunk of concrete, or some other piece of junk. We played every day, all summer long."

Nixon, Del told me, took up golf to please his boss, Eisenhower. After giving Nixon a preemptive pardon for his Watergate shenanigans, Gerald Ford played a round with the "Big Three" of that era, Jack Nicklaus, Arnold Palmer and Gary Player. "I'm a little surprised," said Del, "that POTUS doesn't play."

"He favors blood sports," I was only half joking.

Del studied a French fry. "He needs to be careful."

"Yes," I said, so keen on spilling my news about virtual Luscious I completely missed Del's ominous tone.

Del put the French fry in his mouth and swallowed. "I wish he spent more time with the Vice President."

"As you know," I said, "that's a deeply complicated relationship. All I can say is — just having spoken with POTUS — his faith in her is rock solid."

"I hope she feels the same about him."

"Her world still revolves around POTUS," I said. "But I see Luscious growing more independent. She's determined not to let the ambush incapacitate her. Actually," I felt my eyes welling up, "her strength amazes me. I don't know if you are aware of this but…"

I was about to make my play about her virtual candidacy when, incredibly, Del beat me to it: "I fully support her virtual candidacy," he said. "I think it's smart. A good way for her to keep her recovery on track."

I wilted like a cut daffodil. "I'm glad you think so. Luscious thinks the world of you," I lied. "Your support means a great deal to her."

"The presidency has outgrown human capacity," said Del. "We humans are getting smaller, if you know what I mean. The momentum of history, as Henry Adams put it, has outpaced us — and that includes the president, whomever that happens to be. Going virtual will enable Luscious to do a better job."

"I think it's what people want," I agreed. "Someone to make their problems go away."

Del redirected our conversation with the precision of an air traffic controller. "How's the library coming?"

"Sailing it around the world, as POTUS suggested, threw us for a loop at first but we're past that now."

Del smiled, "You're redefining the presidential library the way POTUS redefined the presidency. I want you to know that I look forward to us working together."

Perhaps, I thought, Del Capeheart and I could get along after all. "The carrier has a Ready Room where we'll have an exhibit showing how POTUS represents the culmination of presidential evolution," I practically rolled out a red carpet. "We'd love your input."

"Presidential history as evolution," said Del. "Like the way fish pulled themselves out of the muck and learned to walk on land…"

"If you could help find an interactive way of showing that…"

Del sat back, beaming. "Sounds like fun, Duke." He called for the check. Our burgers went uneaten.

Virtual Luscious proved irresistible to all but the most die-hard humanists. I thought the highlight of her campaign was her first (and only) debate with the three rather hapless jokers dragooned by their respective parties to run against her. Debates are like game shows; the prize is world domination. Since candidates rarely bother to marshal facts or stand by previously held positions, these doings are notable mainly for each contestant's ability to land a put-down or blunder into a blatant faux pas. At their best, debates can be fun, if somewhat stupid, TV.

Luscious's simulacrum was the prototype for the library's Exbots. We were that confident in the technology. The pornography industry paved the way for us — we merely added a discursive dimension. The illusion, if that's what it/she was, played beautifully.

At the debate, where her rivals strode stolidly to their marks, Exbot Luscious shimmered. She was bright, tender, even a little moist. Her eyes scanned the audience, found the appropriate camera and effortlessly focused, connecting with the millions viewing on their personal devices. Her voice was flutelike, infused with authority and a modicum of humor. She gestured like a dancer. Since she was wirelessly connected to a brace of the world's most formidable search engines, her command of information was instantaneously encyclopedic.

Luscious and I watched the debate at the Naval Observatory. Though still undergoing physical therapy, not to mention an arsenal of daily medications for pain, to enable sleep and facilitate mental clarity, Luscious was a decent approximation of her old self. We sat beside one another on a sofa upholstered with early American imagery: eagles, flintlock rifles and fifes and drums. An orderly in dress whites served popcorn in a cut glass bowl. We washed it down with ginger ale.

Luscious was transfixed by her performance. When the moderator — Dick Manx of PublicMarketStar — asked whether a virtual President could be counted on to celebrate her country's wins and mourn its losses with empathy, virtual Luscious answered by quoting part of Portia's famous speech from *The Merchant of Venice*: "The quality of mercy is not strained. It droppeth like the gentle rain from heaven…" The Luscious sitting next to me whispered, "That's good."

"It's Shakespeare. We should read it," I said without thinking how ridiculously difficult that would be. She nodded without taking her eyes from the screen, took a handful of popcorn and successfully conveyed most of it to her mouth.

At the debate's conclusion, virtual Luscious glided among the other candidates, graciously offering her hand, modestly accepting praise and happily pointing to supporters (Billy and Del Capeheart among them) in the audience. Meanwhile, at the Naval Observatory, the other Luscious's phone tingled. It was POTUS; I heard his voice crackling as she held the device beside her ear. "Thank you, Daddy," she said. And then: "Thank you," followed by, "You have sweet dreams too."

Luscious placed the phone between us on the sofa. She looked exhausted — and relieved. "He wants to see you in the morning."

I was escorted to the Presidential living quarters by a quartet of Secret Service agents — one in front of me, one behind, with one on either side. It was like flying amongst a flock of weaponized geese. Hyper-security was imposed after the State of the Union attack. Heavily armed men and women, wearing ear buds and infrared goggles, were on permanent alert throughout the District. You saw them on street corners, in cafes and lingering near attractions like the National Museum of African American History and Maya Lin's memorial to the tens of thousands killed in Vietnam. The reassurance experienced by tourists who happened to see agents unceremoniously hustling pedestrians into one of a multitude of unmarked vans trolling city streets made the expense this extra vigilance entailed worth it.

Nova Reynard greeted me at the threshold to POTUS's morning room. Her security clearance was now apparently golden. "Hello, Duke!" she beamed. "Would you like coffee or juice?"

Before I could reply, here came POTUS, buffed and coiffed, a boyish smile enlivening the lines beginning to encroach on either side of his face like fleshy parentheses. "Have you seen the reviews?" he practically gushed, grabbing newspapers off a neo-classic, Sheraton style buffet table. "*The New York Times* says, 'a home run!' 'Formidable,' according to the *Wall Street Journal*. And the *Washington Post* calls the Vice President's performance 'disarming,' whatever the hell that means. Basically, Duke, our girl was a knockout. No contest!"

"The verisimilitude and intellectual command were pretty great," I agreed.

"The veri-wha?" POTUS made googly eyes. "I can hardly wait to see all my exes!" He clapped his hands and turned to Nova, "Not to worry, darling. How about a mimosa, Duke?"

"Coffee's fine," I said.

We sat by a window overlooking the south lawn. Teddy Roosevelt's tennis court, Bill Clinton's putting green and the minefield leading up to steel and concrete ramparts blockading the grounds from the National Mall were all in view. "I wanted to talk to you, Duke, because I've had an idea about Mondo POTUS — a flag. We need a flag. A ship should have a flag, don't you think?"

Coffee scalded the roof of my mouth. I nodded my head and reached for a glass of water. "There's the American flag…"

POTUS wagged his head at me. "Nova's idea. Tell the man, darling."

"I was looking at an old dollar bill the other day," said Nova. "You know, the paper kind with a picture of a pyramid on the back? And that eye?" She glanced at POTUS and I thought I saw her blush, "For a second it reminded me of you-know-who. The way he's able to see our country."

POTUS chuckled and pretended to sing: "I know if you are sleeping. I know if you're awake. I know if you've been bad or good — so be BAD for goodness' sake!" He leaned over and gave Nova a kiss on the cheek. "That's so fucking true. I swear."

"So," Nova continued, "I thought, shouldn't the President have a flag of his own?" She produced a piece of drawing paper, with a sketch showing the Eye of Providence. Instead of a pyramid, as on the currency, it sat atop a gold star.

"I see you've substituted a star for the pyramid," I said.

"Yes!" exclaimed Nova. "For our country. And because POTUS is such a star."

"Jesus," said POTUS, grinning like a pit bull. "See what I'm up against?"

"What are the other colors," I asked.

"Blue and red," said POTUS. "Except for the gold star. I think gold is more dramatic than white."

"More royal," said Nova.

"Dramatic," said POTUS. "I like this because in addition to being decorative, the flag design can be the basis for a logo we can use in marketing the hotel piece. How many rooms again, Duke?"

"Fifty, sir, one for every state."

POTUS sipped his sparkling apple juice, considering. "That's not as many as I thought."

"Every room will have a porthole."

He grunted. "How's Luscious? Was she happy last night?"

"She was touched by your call."

"I loved it when she quoted Shakespeare. The guy in the *Post* called it 'Kennedyesque.'"

"High praise," I said.

"I just want Luscious to be happy about this. About being the next President. I want her to believe that as far as I'm concerned, there's no difference between the person she saw on TV last night, and her. I mean, what we saw last night would not have been possible without Luscious. But we're more than this," said POTUS, slapping his chest like a bongo drum.

"Age is just a number," piped Nova.

"That's right," said POTUS. "Thanks to Age Enabling I could probably keep on being President forever. Not that I want to."

"Luscious sees the benefit of having an avatar out there," I said. "But I hope the time will come when she is comfortable enough to appear in her own skin."

POTUS gave me a look. "You think?"

"She's a hero."

"Yes, I know."

"You should come visit," I said. "Both of you. She'd love it."

POTUS looked at Nova. "Let's have some eggs."

HOUR 13:
ORIGIN STORY

Round and round I go…And where I stop? Telling all, remembering everything that's happened, takes longer than I thought. Lucky for me it's a big ocean. But what, I wonder, is Luscious waiting for? I keep expecting her Palace Guard to come swooping in with their grappling hooks. Could it be she's stopped caring about me? That is my worst fear. And greatest hope. Maybe she is listening! The two of us entwined in history's most twisted slumber party.

The conceptual elements for Mondo POTUS were coming together. Separate galleries would be devoted to the events and accomplishments of each term. Immersive media would transport visitors to a battlefield in the Venezuelan War; remind them of the miseries and insecurity of having to hold down a job; inspire greater appreciation (if that was possible) for civic spectatorship; and make fun of the gross inefficiencies of the country's political and journalistic institutions under the old constitution.

Extensive displays celebrated POTUS's lifestyle: his entrepreneurship; business triumphs; friendships with sports stars, entertainment artists and billionaires. Space was reserved for his impact on fashion (all that velour!) and, of course, his passion for classic movies — a screening room modeled on the White House theater, with a daily schedule of his favorites, provided by the Library of Congress.

His Nobel Peace Prize for terminating tensions in the Middle East through "Neutron Diplomacy" — making the region uninhabitable for people while preserving its ancient cultural sites, what diplomats termed "the Lasting Compromise" — was commemorated with a shrine atop the aircraft carrier's Flag Bridge.

Billy's exhibit included baby pix; the lacrosse team stick and mouth guard he used in boarding school; a pictorial record of his vintage sports car collection (he refused to donate any of the real things, despite

Veronica's pleading) and, best of all, an original portrait/installation by renowned Icelandic artist Brrrrm, rendered in mucilage, dried fruit, sand and warm water (estimated value: $15 million).

I think I've mentioned the heroic Luscious wing...

And the Exbots! Our tirelessly glamorous greeters and guides patrolled the various decks, offering their ultimate Insider's perspective on the life and lovestyle of our most tremendous President.

If you are wondering what, if any, part of our design functioned as an actual library — the "growing organism" referred to by Ranganathan — that mission was to be fulfilled digitally, through an interactive archive of trademarked POTUS speeches, press conferences, interviews, personal appearances, walk-ons from assorted television series and rallies (cross referenced by location, date, key words and level of significance as measured on a scale from 1 to 5, with 1 indicating "Transformative" and 5 "Educational"). Visitors accessed the archive via a bank of touch screen monitors located on the carrier's Primary Flight Control deck for an affordable user fee.

What was missing, Veronica Tu told me one morning as she attempted to rub away the dark scallops beneath her eyes, was material dealing with the President's childhood. "There's nothing," she yawned. "It's weird."

I ran my fingers through my Age-Enabled hair. "What do you mean *nothing*?"

"There are no baby pictures or memorabilia. No family stories. No family, as far as I can tell."

Though every other president made the most of an origin story, from Washington chopping down a cherry tree to Clinton's standing up to his abusive stepfather in a town called Hope, POTUS eschewed such stuff. No one had questioned him about this — the rush of events kept carrying us forward, into the future, leaving the past and our collective impatience with its legacy of institutional dysfunction and human misadventure behind. Apart from a few cursory snapshots (in which he was always the sole subject), like POTUS as a little boy, wearing a cowboy vest and hat, in front of a scrawny Christmas tree, or in cap and gown, posing on a nondescript suburban sidewalk prior to his high school graduation, our President's past was largely unexplored.

"People love that kind of content," continued Veronica. "It would be nice to have something. Anything! We still have plenty of space; I think using childhood imagery to decorate the hotel rooms would be so cute."

She was right, of course. What's more, biographers, authorized and otherwise, were doubtless trying to beat us to it; I knew Del Capeheart was on the case. Best we get there with our version first. "OK," I said. "I'll see what I can find out."

The shortest distance being between two points, my first call was to POTUS himself. As usual, I left a message requesting a meeting. Surely, I thought, a man that self-conscious would have a trove of material we could use. I imagined a storage facility in New Jersey, packed with lovingly wrapped baby books, preschool art and hand-scrawled book reports. Days passed; my request for a meeting went unanswered. I attributed this lack of response to an abrupt confluence of events: another breakdown in mutual infrastructure negotiations with the Chinese and the recurrence of annoying guerrilla activity along the U.S.-Canadian border.

I turned to Luscious.

She didn't seem to comprehend what I wanted. Daddy was an open book, she said. A book that began, as far as she was concerned, when she was born.

"But what about before?" I asked her.

Her good eye widened. She raised a finger to her lips and beckoned me to follow as she pushed herself up from the loveseat in her study at the Naval Observatory and limped across the plush carpet toward an ensuite bathroom. Once inside, our images multiplied exponentially by mirrors (evoking Orson Welles' *The Lady From Shanghai*), Luscious opened the faucet full blast (another cinematic touch) to prevent our being overheard. "There are secrets," she whispered.

"Secrets?"

"He doesn't talk about it. He always changes the subject."

"What about his parents? Your grandparents?"

"Dead. Never met them."

"OK…"

"He was an only child — like you, Duke."

"So there's no one?"

Luscious nodded. "You might talk to Billy."

"Billy?" I reached around her and turned off the tap; steam was making the implants on my corneas misty.

Luscious brushed by me, indicating our conversation was over. I could not resist kissing her reconstructed cheek as she reached for the door. She leaned into me and we stood there for maybe two seconds.

I met Billy for a late lunch in the garden-level restaurant at the Tabard Inn, an eccentric old boutique hotel near Dupont Circle favored by aging media types. The hour was such that most of the midday crowd had cleared out; Billy bought added privacy by passing the concierge $1,000 to share among the staff. Members of his heavyset entourage obtrusively positioned themselves at nearby tables, where they nursed glasses of iced mineral water.

Luscious, Billy said, had told him what I wanted. This appeared to please him the way a blind mouse pleases a bored house cat. He intended to take his time. After a round of Papaya Collins cocktails, followed by oxtail soup, duck confit salad and a bottle of Prosecco, he opened up. "Dad had no childhood," he sniggered, "he was raised by wolves."

"C'mon, Billy."

"The funny thing is, it's almost true!"

"I don't understand."

"Well, neither did I," said Billy. "At first. It took Del Capeheart. He is how I know any of this stuff — about my own father."

"Del Capeheart?"

"He's writing a book. I thought you knew."

I tried to cover my discomfort by cracking the caramelized surface of a crème brulee. That Del was working on a book about the President went without saying — he was our Arthur Schlesinger — but his failure to mention any new research nuggets at our Congressional lunch struck me now as being more than a little coy.

"For instance," said Billy, "I didn't know Dad was born in southern Indiana."

"Wait," I said, "I was born in Indiana."

"Dad was born in a town called Madison. It's on the Ohio River. Irene Dunne lived there — you know, she starred in *The Awful Truth* with Cary Grant? And Frank Sinatra shot *Some Came Running* in Madison with Dean Martin and Shirley MacLaine." Billy shook his head, as if in wonder at the improbability of so many larger-than-life Americans haunting such an obscure burg. "I think Dad deleted it from his memory bank."

"Why do you say that?"

"He never really knew his mother. She died when he was a baby. Then his father handed him off to a childless brother. That brother, Dad's uncle, is the one who left him the radio stations."

"Do we know what happened to his father?"

Billy licked his lips. "Del's looking into it."

"It's sad," I said. "But nothing to be ashamed of. I don't see why he wants to keep this under wraps."

"Unless," said Billy, "my grandparents were serial killers. Or Liberals! It's not how POTUS wants to be remembered." He blew his nose into his napkin, which he crumpled into a ball and set atop his plate, where it blossomed, like a sticky flower.

"But," I said, "when Del publishes this material…"

"He won't. He's promised." Billy indicated his entourage with a tilt of his head, "This is strictly a family history, Duke."

Flummoxed. That's how I felt after my lunch with Billy. Nobody, I realized, was being straight with me. Not POTUS —though this was true to form: his was the most assiduously crafted personal brand in the world. Nor Luscious — but she, I told myself, was shell shocked. As for Billy, despite his teasing manner, I guessed he knew less than he let on. It was Del Capeheart's duplicity that got my goat. What else was he holding back?

I found him in his office, meditating on his stellar view of the Washington Monument. A faintly rhythmic wheezing indicated he was doing deep breathing exercises.

"What the fuck, Del!"

He swiveled to face me, a low temperature smile not quite covering his surprise at my salty language.

"Why didn't you tell me about POTUS's family origins?"

"You didn't ask me."

"I thought we were colleagues."

"We are, Duke."

The office walls in the Eisenhower had been reconfigured so many times they were little more than drywall. Instead of raising my voice, I hissed: "What else are you holding back on me?"

Del splayed the fingers of his enormous hands across the top of his desk and took a deep breath. "Because you can't use what I've got."

"Don't you think I should be the judge of that?"

"Only if you want to blow your relationship with the First Family into itty bitty pieces. You're a made man, Duke. Though it hurts me a little to say it, I envy you."

I was still standing. Del stared me up and down, finally said, "Close the fucking door and take a seat." Then: "I understand Billy told you about POTUS being born down there in Madison."

I nodded.

"That his mother died and his dad took off?"

"That was as much as he said you had."

"When last we spoke of POTUS's origins, yes."

"Is there more?"

I thought I detected a twinkle in Del's eye. "Look," I pressed him, "shouldn't I know what you've got? We need to be prepared for when it gets out — which we both know is bound to happen."

"Probably," Del nodded. "Probably. Did you know POTUS has a sister?"

"He's an only child!"

Del shook his head. "He's a twin. When POTUS was born, his mother also gave birth to a baby girl. It's like there were two of him — one male, one female."

I felt the implications piling up behind my forehead. "Where is she? Who is she?"

"Dunno," Del shrugged. "POTUS's dad apparently took her with him."

"What's his story?"

"Interesting case. A real joker. POTUS's parents were itinerant. Outwardly, they might have seemed like what used to be called hippies, only without the white privilege. They weren't about changing the world. It was all sex and drugs as far as they were concerned. All counter, no culture. When the dad's old lady died, being stuck with a couple of kids was too much for him."

"But he kept the little girl?"

"It probably worked for him, like having a dog. They went first to Cincinnati, where he lands a job with, now get this: Larry Flynt."

"*Hustler* magazine?"

"The same! Dad makes himself useful: driver, butler, gofer; picks up models at the airport, scrubs the hot tub, serves drinks."

"Where's POTUS's sister?"

"Her name is Merrie, by the way. Just like *Merrie Melodies* in the Warner Brothers cartoons? She's there. Going to Catholic school on Larry Flynt's dime. Everything's cool until Flynt gets shot in '78, winds up in a wheelchair with a serious painkiller habit. Dad decides to get out of Cincinnati. Finds a job in Nashville, leading tours of RCA Studio B for the Country Music Hall of Fame. Seems like a better perch for Merrie, as she's starting to mature. I mean, compared to *Hustler*. In any event, Dad finally croaks after a Hank Williams, Jr. concert, leaving Merrie on her own at the age of…" Del counted on his fingers, "seventeen, if I'm not mistaken."

"Where is she now?"

Del shrugged. "I'm trying to find out, but Dad never remarried so there are no familial third parties to interview. Given that she's the President's sister, you'd think she'd have surfaced by now, made a claim or sold her story but there's none of that. Trail's cold as a dead snake."

I folded my arms across my chest, trying to fend off what I'd just heard. "And nobody knows about any of this?"

"I do," said Del. "Billy knows there was a sister, who's probably dead. We decided Luscious doesn't need to know any of this yet — not while she's still recovering and in the midst of her election campaign. Why create another level of stress she can't do anything about?"

"What about POTUS? Where's he in all this?"

Del chuckled. "The family part of POTUS's brain has zero bandwidth. He doesn't talk about it. Billy tried to broach it and POTUS spilled sparkling apple juice all over Billy's white jeans. Made it look like Billy'd pee'd himself. POTUS pretended it was an accident. I haven't brought it up with him. Yet."

"Will you?"

"Someday I'll have to. I can't write his life story without trying to get him on the record. But it occurs to me that you might bring it up with him."

I shook my head, "My work's about launching Mondo POTUS. That's it. Let's agree this conversation never happened."

Del smiled. "You see, Mutz? I've got your back."

I've been asked what, besides old movies, POTUS really liked? Favorite bands, for instance. Teams he rooted for. Restaurants, even. Heroes — who did he look up to?

Material like this could easily have accounted for hundreds of running feet of content aboard Mondo POTUS. Displayed our leader's private side. But when it came to that, POTUS was elusive. He had no favorite bands; associating his most vivid memories with popular songs never occurred to him. He thought rooting for any team that didn't win was a waste of energy. As for food, if POTUS heard a particular dish was the best or most talked about, he might try it — otherwise he was content with grilled cheese and a handful of peanuts. Immediacy was his thing. Old school concepts like loyalty, tradition, or even love implied commitment and commitment is slow. POTUS was a heat seeker. The present, for him, was continuous.

Life in the continuous present doesn't erase history, it sensationalizes it. As I've said, old movies enlivened history for POTUS. In his eyes, Abraham Lincoln was indistinguishable from Henry Fonda, the iconic movie star who played Honest Abe in *Young Mister Lincoln*. For POTUS, the face on the screen and the sixteenth President were one and the same. Not only that, Lincoln/Fonda was an American amalgamation that POTUS tracked through the Dust Bowl in *The Grapes of Wrath*; during World War II in *Mister Roberts*; and to the brink of nuclear annihilation in *Fail Safe* (where Lincoln/Fonda embodied another, albeit mid-20th Century modern, President of the United States). Lincoln/Fonda was a cowboy who witnessed a lynching in *The Ox-Bow Incident*; Marshall Wyatt Earp in *My Darling Clementine*; and a herpetologist lucky enough to be seduced by Barbara Stanwyck in *The Lady Eve*.

I know for a fact POTUS (accompanied by the Joint Chiefs, the Secretary of State and the heads of the National Security Agency and the CIA) watched a pristine black and white print of *The Longest Day* the night before launching their invasion of Venezuela. POTUS sat through all 178 minutes and, when the credits rolled over the image of an empty helmet tipped upside down on a Normandy beach, he gave the projectionist two thumbs up. Lincoln/Fonda, by the way, was shown leading the American assault on Utah Beach.

I've said POTUS insisted on including a movie theater aboard Mondo POTUS. It replicated the White House screening room, but with more seating. Home screening systems, not to mention the fear of infectious disease, had practically rendered movie theaters obsolete but he was not deterred. "People will see movies here the way they're meant to be seen," he said, "On a silver screen."

POTUS locked on to whatever (or whoever) was right in front of him. This, I suppose, explains all those exes. It might even account for my career: I happened to be the right face at the right time. What he did not like: contemplation. He waved away analysis, disdainfully pointing out that its root word was *anal*. "Get your head out of your ass," he'd growl at some second-guessing general or intellectual bureaucrat. Critics in the early days wondered if, maybe, this indicated a form of attention deficit disorder. Most of us found it disarmingly selfless. There's a Zen saying, "If you meet the Buddha on the road, kill him." That was POTUS. As in-the-moment as it gets.

Veronica Tu was downcast when I told her — without going into detail — that dedicating a section of Mondo POTUS to POTUS the Younger was probably impossible. "We have to stick," I said, "to the many accomplishments of his Administration."

"What a lost opportunity," she pouted.

"Yes," I said. "Someday we might mount a special exhibition." I secretly congratulated myself on validating her original idea, holding out hope for the future and, implicitly, suggesting her job was safe. Sure enough, her eyes brightened with readiness.

"We can do more with his Nobel win," she said. "Make the neutron bomb a motif!"

All I needed to say was: "Brilliant."

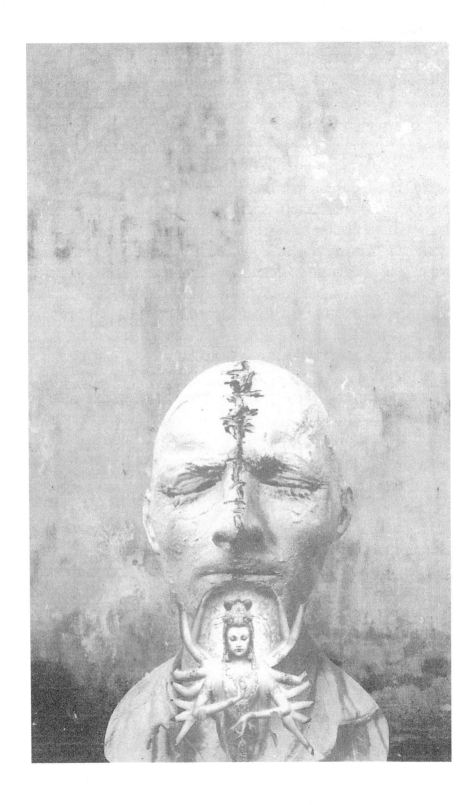

HOUR 14:
MANIACAL ZITHER MUSIC

Election day was fast approaching. Although Luscious's ascent (virtual and otherwise) to the Oval Office was never truly in doubt, the country's quadrennial awards show cum job interview marking, in this case, the transition from father to daughter had its share of jitters. That some cranky opposition party members and a few aging pundits considered the succession's dynastic aspect hubristic was not surprising. Our position was: Like it or lump it.

Most Americans would happily have allowed POTUS a fourth term and skipped voting altogether. Indeed, some wondered why, if a virtual Luscious could make the grade, a virtually immortal POTUS couldn't be engineered to hold office…forever! In response, POTUS smiled in that half self-deprecating way of his and said, "not on my watch," or, "that's very flattering," or "probably not what the Founders intended."

POTUS tended to think he had accomplished all a man in a scientifically enabled human span could. Transformed not just the presidency, but society itself. Brought us up to date. Now, he said, all he wanted was to spend more quality time with his sweet Nova.

Luscious's rehab continued apace. She walked without grabbing on to the backs of chairs or other nearby pieces of furniture. She no longer left telltale palm prints on the Colonial Williamsburg wallpaper in the hallways of the Naval Observatory. When she spoke, it was with authority — albeit a slight slur that, I assured her, would be imitated by social butterflies from Nashville to Las Vegas.

I continued reading to her. We called these bedtime sittings our "lullaby sessions." Having exhausted Nancy Drew, we took up the Western novels of Louis L'Amour. Something about the frontier appealed to Luscious; she started wearing a buckskin jacket with intricate beadwork on the back displaying a Thunderbird, the Native American symbol of power, protection and strength. One night, following a session of equine therapy, she confided to me that, "the world really does look different from the back of a horse." We were reading L'Amour's *How the West Was Won*, a novelization based on the 1962 wide screen Cinerama blockbuster, starring John Wayne, James Stewart, Debbie Reynolds and, of course, Abraham Lincoln's doppelganger, Henry Fonda (playing a buffalo hunter). I couldn't help thinking her father would have preferred the movie, projected as originally intended, on three synchronized screens.

There were no October surprises before the election. The media, as per its mandate, made sure the most popular candidate (Luscious) received the most attention. As election day approached, speculation grew over whether or not Luscious herself would make a public appearance — while casting her vote and/or for a victory speech once the returns were counted. A few gadflies, sniping from the relative obscurity afforded by the more outre streaming platforms, suggested Luscious feared her disfigurement might shake the confidence of her biggest financial backers. "When, Madam Vice President, will we see the real you?" a self-important journo demanded of Luscious's simulacrum at the Next Coast Festival in Omaha.

Virtual Luscious sighed. Then launched into a brief but cogent reflection on the nature of reality and Heisenberg's Uncertainty Principle. She was tart as an unsweetened slice of Key Lime pie. "I was good there," the real Luscious said to me, as we watched the press conference at home. "What's an uncertainty principle?"

It was finally decided that real Luscious's first public appearance should take place on election night. I, POTUS made clear, had better be standing by her side. "You being there," he said, "will say to the world, 'She's fine. In fact, she's fine enough to marry,' which, if we announce your engagement there, at the same time, will make it the greatest election night ever. Twice as nice!"

"Twice as nice?"

"Winning and love," grinned POTUS. "It'll be a real treat for everybody. You know I'd prefer it if you proposed right there, in the middle of all the cheering and confetti, but that might be a little much. I'm thinking of Luscious, you see. On the other hand, having the two of you announce your wedding, sharing your good news on top of a great victory, sort of normalizes her."

The months since the ambush had been the most fulfilling of my entire life. The bond between Luscious and me was more real than it had ever been — a codependency made in heaven, or so I thought. She depended on me and I needed her more deeply than I was capable of saying. Neither of us had ever mentioned marriage. I allowed her father's/my boss's early promptings to gently sink, like compost, into the loam of my subconscious. I was content with our situation. Didn't want to be the story, as they say. I also feared how Luscious might react if she was pushed to make a commitment. Whatever we were, I was reluctant to test it.

On the day after Halloween, POTUS was driven in a motorcade to the Naval Observatory for a face-to-face with Luscious. I wasn't there; didn't see and couldn't gauge the expression that crossed his tanning peptide-treated brow as he laid eyes on his actual daughter for the first time in weeks. Did her appearance startle him? Make him want to reach out and hold her? Break his heart? Maybe it turned him on! As he leaned in close to her shell-like ear, urgently outlining the grand scheme he had concocted for us, I can imagine him feeling a transgressive rush.

And what did my dear Luscious do? I believe she went very still. I imagine her head cocked slightly, beagle-like and her eyes, both of them, fixed upon a picture hanging on the wall: a nautical lithograph depicting the warship Bonhomme Richard during its Revolutionary War sea battle with the British frigate Serapis. This, America's first naval victory, was where John Paul Jones, his ship blown to bits, with dead and dying sailors lying at his feet, uttered the immortal words: "I have not yet begun to fight!"

She heard POTUS make his pitch. About marrying me. Then she asked him: "What does Duke think?"

"Oh, he's all over it," said POTUS, "loves the idea. He's crazy about you, you know."

"Well," she said, without taking her eyes from the raging sea battle pictured on the wall, "I'd like to talk to him about it."

Although somewhat surprised by anything other than instant acquiescence from his daughter, POTUS could see how, for the moment, the gravity of his brilliant idea might gum up her neural pathways. He'd been married a few times himself, after all. So he offered up his most solicitous smile — the same one he'd used to such great effect on the British Prime Minister.

A few minutes later, he called me from the back of his armor-plated limousine. "I've talked to Luscious," he said.

"What did you say to her?"

"I told her about our plan."

How about that? The President of the United States, the Most Powerful Person in the World, proposing marriage on my behalf! Never having proposed to anybody myself, I wondered what it felt like.

"She's fine," said POTUS, adding: "Talk about a match made in heaven!"

"What did she say?"

"She wants to talk. To you. Man up...son. You're about to be a very lucky guy."

The Washington Nationals had just won baseball's World Series. Our football team, the Commanders, was undefeated. In a few days the country would enjoy a "seamless" transition of power, as a sitting President handed the keys to the White House to a woman who happened to be his daughter. I, Duke Mutz of Hammond, Indiana, would be part of this spectacle —standing there on stage as my bride-to-be took her place in history, acknowledging her victory and promising the American people all the winning and righteous vengeance they deserved. It looked to be the greatest engagement party ever.

I was sitting at my desk, contemplating the collection of photographs hanging on my office wall: me, standing next to POTUS on his yacht in Palm Beach; me, pretending to cower as POTUS lifted a foam rubber boulder over my head at Universal Studios in Atlanta; me, in a flak jacket and too-small helmet, with POTUS in Venezuela; me, at the first Inaugural Ball, dancing with Luscious. I got up and put my face close to that last one, squinted to try and see every detail, to relive the moment. The orchestra was playing a waltz, the only sort of formal dance my two left feet were capable of approximating. My close-up reflection bounced back at me from the glass, scowling with concentration. On that night, still flush with the incomprehensibility of victory, I danced as if I'd crossed a finish line, not appreciating that this was just the beginning.

The more I thought of myself as married, the more I liked the idea. It was the novelty of it, I told myself, that threw me for a loop at first. You see I had never thought of myself as "the marrying kind." I considered myself more a Gig Young type, the guy you see playing second lead in one of Douglas Sirk's romantic melodramas. Gig's the one with the crooked smile who watches wistfully as the girl he loves drives off with Rock Hudson. But when I stepped back and took a look at my situation from 50,000 feet, I could see I'd been married to POTUS and his family for most of my adult life. This was what he'd been trying to tell me the night we watched *Northwest Passage* in the White House screening room.

And I'd been acting like a teenager! Bucking a great idea because Dad thought of it first.

Was POTUS my surrogate Old Man? We never discussed our both being fatherless children; yet, from the beginning of our knowing one another, POTUS included me in his family circle, letting me play Tom Hagen — the adopted son — from The Godfather. I told myself he and I were colleagues, collaborators, maybe even friends. It never entered my mind that I might be attracted to the man because he fulfilled some unspoken need for a father figure. I didn't permit myself to think of him that way.

The funny thing was that so many Americans had started calling POTUS the Father of their Country. It was as if George Washington never existed. As far as most of us were concerned, America's history started anew with Income for All and the Rebranding. With putting an end to the idea that our country was some kind of civic "experiment." If I had daddy issues, everybody else did, too. Although in my case, POTUS not only embodied America 2.0, he was also about to be my father-in-law.

I think perfection is a crazy concept. It's unnatural. But the more I thought about the union of Luscious with yours truly, the more perfect it seemed to me. Could any couple achieve greater intimacy? I thought of Krupskaya and her partnership with Lenin — me playing Krupskaya (both of us being librarians) and Luscious… in the Lenin part. The platonic nature of our bond only strengthened things for me. "Face it, you big lug," I chided myself, "you're in love with the girl."

A subtropical front was stalled over the lower half of the Eastern Seaboard. It had been raining incessantly for a week. The streets were bubbling sluices of rushing water, sewers gushed their human offload into the Potomac and Anacostia Rivers. I was in my office, rehearsing the proposal of marriage I intended to make personally to Luscious over dinner at the Naval Observatory when a Security Alert informed me the Vice President was in the building and on her way up to see me.

I ducked into my private washroom to assure myself there were no unmasticated remnants of lunch clinging to my dental implants. It was disappointing that I was without flowers, or any other token of esteem, to embellish the pledge I now intended, then and there, to make to my beloved. But this, I told myself, was in keeping with the headlong character of our partnership. There would be time for tokens and gifts — a lifetime! I gave my cuffs a gentle tug.

Luscious was standing with her back to me. She wore a rain-spattered, carbon tinted duster with a broad-brimmed vinyl hat. She turned when she heard me enter the room. Her face looked white as the limestone dome on the Jefferson Memorial. Before I could say hello or greet her in any way, she said:

"There will be no marriage, Duke."

She did not say she was sorry. This, for all of you who don't remember, was the true meaning of love, according to Eric Segal, the academic classicist who published the drugstore novel *Love Story* — later a preposterously popular film — making him rich and, he claimed, ruining his life.

Luscious told me her decision wasn't personal. But, with the election just days away, she admitted to a feeling she had never experienced before; an undomesticated impulse to insert a crack of daylight between herself and her father.

It was me who said, "I'm sorry." I felt light-headed, staggered by how out of control I had allowed this situation to become. I'd let POTUS run away with my imagination and, all of a sudden, a precipice was looming up ahead.

"For what?" asked Luscious, wiping (a tear? I didn't dare let myself think it) at her injured eye.

"I should have proposed to you myself," I said. "The way this happened was unfair. It wasn't right."

She shook her head. "I'm glad you didn't. It wouldn't have changed anything."

Remember Joseph Cotton? Him standing alone as that maniacal zither music plays and Alida Valli walks past him and out of the shot at the end of *The Third Man*? Luscious said it was best if tonight we skipped our reading of Louis L'Amour's Sackett family saga. Little changes in routine so often foretell bigger things to come. Here's the weird bit: Luscious took hold of my hand and shook it — something I don't think she had ever done before. It took me by surprise. As we grasped each other's flesh and fingers, I found myself looking not in her eyes but at our appendages enfolding one another. Her grip was surprisingly firm; it almost kept my heart from breaking.

HOUR 15: INCONGRUOUS SMALL TALK

History, they say, is written by the winners. If so, who will take the time to listen to *my* story — let alone read the transcript? When Luscious let go of my hand and walked out of my office, I felt like a strip of old celluloid, cut from the picture and left on the cutting room floor. I looked around for a sign indicating the life-altering exchange that had just happened. Everything was just as it had been. Those pictures hanging on the wall. My Herman Miller swivel chair. A coffee mug with a cartoon drawing of Teddy Roosevelt in a Rough Rider hat, getting colder on my desk.

Del Capeheart's oversized head appeared within the frame of my still open office doorway like one of those mylar balloons people ritualistically launch to memorialize murdered inner city kids. It was a sitcom moment: The nosy neighbor. "Hey, Mutz," he said. "You look like you've seen a ghost."

"Must be the weather," I lied, glancing toward the rain battering my office window.

"Wet brain," Del nodded. "They say the waves are twenty feet high off Virginia Beach."

Back in Hammond, when I was being bullied by bigger kids, I learned to divert them from beating me up by making incongruous small talk. I asked Del if he surfed.

He, however, would not be distracted. "Did I see the Vice President?"

"A courtesy call," I said.

"Amazing how she's able to be in two places at once," he laughed. "Her virtual candidacy creates a new sort of narrative for historians like me."

"For all of us."

"I wonder what happens if it turns out Americans prefer VL to RL," said Del, using the popular shorthand for Virtual and Real Luscious. "Though when you think about it, they really complement one another." He grinned lasciviously, "One you fuck the other you marry, no?"

When Del grew bored pulling my wings, he said he looked forward to seeing me at the Omni Shoreham on election night, where a gathering was planned to await the returns. I stared at him until he finally left, then grabbed my raincoat, locked the office door and gave myself to the downpour overwhelming the National Mall.

The Mall's spacious gravel walkways were muddy tracks. Tree limbs sagged under the weight of so much precipitation. I could have used a snorkel. By the time I reached the Lincoln Memorial, my pants were soaked to the knees and my $800 pair of handcrafted Milano double monk straps were overflowing.

I made the long climb up the memorial's unforgiving steps to where, three terms ago, Mr. Lincoln's contemplative visage overlooked POTUS, Luscious and Billy. The image of that moment was being installed aboard Mondo POTUS. I wiped the rain from my eyes and regarded Lincoln's kindly face the way Michael Rennie's spaceman, Klaatu, does in *The Day the Earth Stood Still*. Even an alien from another planet could feel the Old Man's compassion.

Lincoln's Washington contemporaries considered him an oddball and worse. For one thing, he was from Illinois — considered the West, the back of beyond in those days. Sophisticates found his habit of turning every conversation into a koan-like parable about some innkeeper, farmer or undertaker he'd known back in Springfield unfunny and annoying. They put up with these tales because Lincoln, much to their chagrin, was President.

What Lincoln's detractors mistook for frontier tomfoolery was actually thinking out loud. Storytelling was his way of untying knotty problems. If he told the same story more than once, it wasn't because he was insufferably uncool (though that's what many in Washington believed) but because he hoped to find a clue, some detail in the telling, that might cast light he hadn't seen before. Maybe that's what I'm trying to do now, telling this story.

I heard someone cough. For a second I wondered if it might be Abe himself. A thickly bearded man was sitting on the cold stone floor, sheltering in a far corner of Lincoln's neoclassical box of memories. He was wrapped in the sort of greasy mufti I took to be a homeless uniform, with one of those flat, woolen caps media coverage made familiar during the Afghan wars. One arm was propped on a fully stuffed black plastic trash bag. He spoke to me:

"You alright?"

Like all seasoned city dwellers, I try not to make eye contact with street people, let alone engage in conversation. Pretend they are invisible and it will be so. If not for the rain, I probably would have turned and fled. But I was soaked and shivering, pathetic even to myself. "Not great," I admitted.

The bearded man nodded. "Sometimes the shit falls so hard, you need a hat."

"Yes," I agreed, recognizing a line from *Body Heat*, the neo noir classic about lust and betrayal. Another movie lover, I thought, an unexpected bond.

"My name's Malone," said the bearded man, not changing his position.

"I'm Mutz."

"Hello, Mutz."

"It's terrible out there," I said, indicating the rain. My voice echoed softly in the great space.

Malone looked around, as if he had just arrived. "It's dry here," he said. "A little drafty. I like the company."

"Lincoln," I said. "Yes."

"Tried to keep the Union in one piece. Looking back, I wonder why he thought that was so important. What he thought Americans had in common. The whole thing was just a big idea. He thought it was worth fighting over."

"He was thinking of the future," I said.

Malone shook his head. "I fought," he said. "In Afghanistan, a long time ago. That was an idea, too. We were making the world safe from terror. But you know what? The world is never safe. Never has been. Never will be. That's the hard truth, man."

Afghanistan, I thought. He might have been fighting there, his back against some bullet-riddled wall, while I sipped my first Luscious at the Breakers in Palm Beach.

"I've seen things," said Malone. "But I'm done seeing that shit now."

His feet were wrapped in rags, like what soldiers wore when they wintered with Washington at Valley Forge. "Here," I said, impulsively loosening the buckles on my sodden Milanos. "They're soaked but you can have them."

Malone was incredulous. "What are you doing? It's raining, man!"

I carried the shoes over to him and set them on the limestone floor. The cold came through the fine acrylic threads of my socks. "Nice meeting you."

"Yeah," said Malone. "You sure about this?"

"I'm done, too," I said before starting down the Memorial steps. They were slippery in my stocking feet. At the bottom I climbed into a Hummingbird and tapped in my address. I was home, shivering, in minutes.

HOUR 16:
A NOTION, BRIEFLY

The 2052 election went as planned. According to Amazon's NoFraud voting subscription system, Luscious swept all the states and territories. Though her showing was pallid in under-populated urban areas, she more than made up for this in the sprawling exurbs once considered farm country. Pundits compared the impact of her virtual candidacy with the advent of political advertising on television and FDR's fireside chats on the radio.

On election night, the real Luscious, dressed in an outfit evoking equal parts geisha and G.I. Joe, was joined on stage by her animated doppelganger. They engaged in scripted banter which was roundly praised by the press for its use of self-deprecating humor to reassure the public that real Luscious was most certainly in charge, while softening whatever consternation her appearance aroused among viewers at home. The evening's high point came when POTUS, beaming behind the Resolute Desk in the Oval Office, was projected on to an enormous screen installed in the Omni Shoreham's ballroom and live streamed across the country and the world.

"How are you honey, I mean Madam President-elect," he mugged to a rapturous ovation that went on and on. Luscious, her lower lip aquiver, clasped her hands above her head like a prize fighter.

I was not there. Chose instead to watch the festivities, semi-recumbent, from the couch in my apartment. Was I sorry for myself? Wishing it was me on stage, playing Luscious's straight man — the new George Burns to her imperial Gracie Allen? I'd be lying if I denied it. Yet never having actually proposed, I took comfort in telling myself I had not been terminally rejected. I had been a notion, briefly.

As ballroom imagery sparkled over my implanted IOLs, I sucked a THC gummi and caught sight of Del Capeheart's silver head towering above the crowd. Billy, wearing a top hat, mingled aggressively among the revelers. History, I thought, has multiple personalities. There's a history of events, like those that engulfed Malone in Afghanistan. But there's another kind of history — the history of what almost happened but didn't. Antihistory. Me.

Veronica Tu leased an abandoned shopping mall in Alexandria, Virginia for the design, fabrication, testing and storage of Mondo POTUS tech. A nondescript architectural dump surrounded by a concrete desert, the place did nothing to alleviate my inner listlessness when I visited a few days after the election. Veronica met me outside the entrance to what had once been an anchor for this obsolete business model, an upscale department store, whose name, Saks Fifth Avenue, was faded but still legible on the building's rust-streaked facade. Veronica wore iridescent orange coveralls. Green plastic goggles dangled round her neck.

"Recovered from the victory party yet?" she asked. "I didn't see you there."

I told her I'd been under the weather.

"It was insane!" She'd gone home with the Secretary of Agriculture. "We fucked 'til neither one of us could make a fist. It was like eating too much fried Twinkies at the State Fair."

"Elections," I said, "can be very sexy."

"We should have them more often!" Veronica led me past dust encrusted display cases in which perfumes and scented emollients had once been arrayed to glamorous effect. We headed deep into the old mall's interior. A battalion of fabricators were using former retail outlets as workshops for the construction of various Mondo POTUS attractions. Testing of animatronic and interactive features, like the Exbots, took place on the broad concrete concourses, where, in another era, motley teens jeered at elderly mall walkers trying to get some exercise.

I recognized Juniper, looking as gorgeously wasted as the night I met her with POTUS at the "Existential Bargains" show in New York City. She slouched in front of a derelict Bed Bath & Beyond, eyes blinking uncontrollably as a pair of technicians hovered, staring intently at palm screens while trying to get her software's rhythms synchronized. "You knew her, right?" Veronica asked me.

"In the old days." Juniper had recorded an album of chansons, made a handful of films (one of which was considered a torture porn classic), designed a forgotten line of handbags and raced greyhounds in Ireland. She had not been publicly photographed for almost thirty years.

"She's jumpy," Veronica called to the technicians, neither of whom acknowledged her. Veronica turned to me, "I'm going to the carrier next week to double check the dimensions on a few of the spaces. Want to come?"

Not so long ago the prospect of a day trip to Hampton Roads would have seemed a lark. Veronica's invitation reminded me how enervated I felt. I barely had the energy to turn her down. On my way back to the city I considered: Maybe my number was finally up. Maybe it was time to exit POTUS world.

The more I thought about it, the more this made sense to me. The transition from one administration to another; Luscious back on her feet; Mondo POTUS in production — I could take a bow, blow some kisses and buy myself a cottage in the Black Hills before real estate there went totally batshit. I might land a seat on a corporate board or two, let my name appear on a think tank's letterhead. It wasn't too soon. POTUS minions with a fraction of my bragging rights were showering the fruited plains with their 3-D resumes.

I lay awake nights thinking about the future. Lost my appetite. Called in sick. That my adult life amounted to little more than a series of fortuitous encounters haunted me. Always saying yes accounted for everything I had. Yet here I was, tempted finally to say no.

I looked out my apartment's kitchen window toward the bare trees on the slopes of Meridian Hill Park. At the top of that park's twelve acres stood a starling-spattered statue honoring a previous bachelor President, James Buchanan — the man whose mess Lincoln inherited. There must have been a time when Buchanan looked like he had the world by the tail. He beat both Stephen Douglas, the "Little Giant" and "the Pathfinder," John C. Fremont to win the presidency in 1856. He was untroubled by slavery; thought it was a matter of states' rights. When some of those states threatened to secede from the Union, Buchanan shrugged. Said the President "can accomplish but little for good or for evil on such a momentous question."

What if he was right? What if the South had simply been allowed to stew in its peculiar juice? If slavery had been given the chance to outlive its usefulness like, say, the Erie Canal? The transcontinental railroad put canals out of business. Share-cropping replaced slavery. The Union prevailed in spite of itself and Buchanan shuffled off to historical oblivion.

Billy said if POTUS wasn't careful, Nova Reynard would kill him with too much sex. "One of these nights he's going to die in her arms," he said over drinks at the Cosmos Club. "I mean, really!"

Now that his dad was a lame duck, whatever inhibitions kept Billy from laughing at the old man's expense appeared to be waning. His expectations regarding a potential role in his sister's Cabinet billowed like a spinnaker on a windy afternoon. Head of Housing and Urban Development — that seemed about right, thought Billy. When I asked if Luscious had promised him this, he admitted they had not actually talked about it. Yet. It was "a brother-sister thing, Duke." The kind of thing that I, being an only child, could never understand.

I wonder, as I rattle on like this, what made me want to unburden myself with Billy about the creeping disaffection I felt about my life, my career, Mondo POTUS. But in that moment, his half-cocked scheming betrayed an ingenuousness I could still find affecting. He reminded me of Lew Ayres, Katherine Hepburn's drunken brother in *Holiday*; a defeated guy who could still be kind of sweet.

It didn't take long for me to figure out that Billy had never been aware of the marriage POTUS intended for Luscious and me. He volunteered nothing in the way of condolence, commiseration or even gossip. Instead, he waxed on about his father's amorous adventures and his hope that Beyonce might change her mind and agree to host the climactic Inaugural Ball — one of five being planned. "She's the National Poet," said Billy, probably not fully understanding what Poet Laureate meant. "I know she hasn't danced in decades but I think she might recite something. It would mean so much to Luscious. There could be a Medal of Freedom in it for her."

As for Nova, apart from the danger she posed to POTUS's artificial heart, Billy found her, "funny, charming, a lucky break for Dad. Tons better for him than another world leader, or some striver from the media pool. Del and I had a bowling night with them last Saturday."

"Oh?" I roused myself. "Who won?"

"She did. I mean, she and Dad. Neither he nor I were any good. She and Del, on the other hand, killed. Del has such long arms." Billy shook his head in awe.

"What does Del think of Nova?"

"He thinks she's…busy. But he appreciates her interest in history. She seems quite keen about Dad's legacy. She asked Del a lot of questions about his research. And Mondo POTUS."

My antennae began to twitch. "What did he say about Mondo POTUS?"

Billy offered an indulgent smile. "I know you two get a little competitive, but he's for it. You have to remember that Del's a traditionalist. You're more avant-garde."

"I'm a librarian, Billy."

"Whatever. Nova's got some interesting ideas about marketing Mondo POTUS. You should call her."

She called me! Which was handy because being in a funk, I was having trouble communicating the way I was supposed to. Though constantly being importuned, called upon, or begged for decisions, opinions and advice, I was shutting down. What should have thrilled me only made me tired. Here I was living every hustler's dream: being not just busy, but too busy to care about anything besides work — yet all I wanted to do was sleep. I was in the clutches of something other people took achiever drugs to try and fix.

The White House was on Line #1. Part of my brain was still susceptible to pomp and circumstance because my forehead tingled. I touched ACCEPT expecting to hear the voice of POTUS; it was Nova: "Duke Mutz, what does a girl have to do?" She laughed — her way of cutting through the clutter. She said she'd been hearing great things about Mondo POTUS. Did I have time to go for a walk-and-talk?

We met near the red brick battlements of the old Smithsonian Castle on Independence Avenue. The weather was dank and windy; Nova wrapped herself in a long faux fur coat, which made her seem taller than I remembered. She bought us plant-based sandwiches ("my treat") from a brushed steel jackfruit wagon, spraying hers with THC infused harissa sauce, which she urged me to try.

"Let's go to the Air and Space Museum," she said between bites. "This weather's nasty and I love what they've done with the Inner Space Portal."

We ate as we walked the short distance, pausing for the traffic light to change on Seventh Avenue. Nova looked down at me — her height, I realized, was accentuated by a pair of high-heeled boots — saying: "POTUS is worried about you, Duke. Is everything OK?"

I wolfed down a mouthful of shredded jackfruit, getting a salty sweet flavor combo I associated with the Obama years. "Well," I said — and the light changed.

"Hold that thought," Nova chuckled.

The Air and Space Museum was, as usual, a giant riot of impossibly large flying objects, many of them suspended from the ceiling, as if the enormous hall was an elephantine hobby shop. I followed Nova as she snaked her way to an elevator that took us two floors up to the gallery devoted to Inner Space.

Created during POTUS's first term, after yet another aborted mission to Mars — the Inner Space Portal was designed to reimagine the "deep state" of human exploration. Rather than obsessing about worlds outside ourselves, ISP installations encouraged looking within, at consciousness itself. A public private partnership between Disney, NASA, and the American Pharmaceutical Association, the ISP combined dimension conflating compositions of light and shadow with interactive animations.

The THC in our sandwiches was beginning to make itself felt in subtle but gratifying ways. Nova and I found a bench in an unoccupied gallery where light was being used to make our perception of the space intimate and limitless. Nova giggled. "You were about to tell me something."

I extended my arms fully in front of me, expecting to touch a wall I thought was there but wasn't. All I felt was ventilated air, like down, drifting across my fingertips. "I've been a little depressed."

Nova startled me. "Because Luscious turned you down?"

"How did you know?"

"POTUS tells me everything. He can't help himself. It sounds like he put you both in an awkward position. He knows it. He's impetuous."

I tasted the light. It was like honeysuckle fog. "I don't blame him," I said. "But I feel like my time is up. Like my work is done."

"Your work? You mean Mondo POTUS?"

I nodded.

"There are miles to go, Duke. POTUS needs you."

"I don't know about that."

"It's what he wants. He trusts you." Nova's gloved hand briefly touched mine. "So do I."

I wanted to say something funny here. Lighten the mood and make Nova laugh. My old *modus operandi*. But I felt myself tensing up.

"The peaceful transition of power isn't as predictable as some people like to make it seem," said Nova. "And when one president is as much a part of his country's brand identity as POTUS, it takes extra effort — even if the successor is part of the family. People get jumpy. They might do things. Things they could regret."

"Are you talking about me?"

Nova shook her head. "I'm talking about what we need to avoid, Duke. POTUS made the America people wanted; I don't think we need to start over again, do you?"

"I'm the one who needs a fresh start."

"Oh, Duke. You're Mr. North Star."

How enchanting, I thought, to be sitting here beside this lovely creature. I hazarded a sidelong glance. Nova's skin seemed so present and alive. It reminded me of the back of Luscious's neck when we lay like spoons during our first night at the Breakers.

"This room is amazing," I said.

"Wonderful, isn't it?"

"Yes."

"Think how wonderful Mondo POTUS will be. Everyone will be so proud."

"You really think so?"

"It will be the ultimate American destination, Duke."

"Del Capeheart will say it doesn't have enough history."

Nova touched my wrist. "Del will be happy to see his books for sale in your gift shop."

Everything we were saying seemed like code for something else.

"Del can write whatever he wants," said Nova. "But if he thinks he's bigger than his subject, he's mistaken."

Lucky POTUS, I thought. Nova was more than beautiful. We were connecting in a way I found providential. "Thank you," I said.

"For what?"

"For making me feel like I'm still in the game."

"The game is on, Duke." Nova got to her feet and stretched. Subaqueous light darkened her features, though her voice sounded bright. "I love it here," she said.

"Yes," I agreed, "I could sit here all afternoon."

Nova laughed. "I mean our Nation's Capital, Washington, D.C. — like it says on all the pennants and mousepads they sell to tourists."

Looking up at her, seeing the light emanating from her eyes, made me glad. "What do you love about it?"

"It feels like home."

It was my turn to stand. I wanted to embrace Nova, even kiss her

— anything to demolish the space between us. I thought of Luscious; all our platonic nights filled with desire and longing. How sometimes I wanted to crush her beauty by way of paying tribute to it.

Then I wondered: had Nova called me because she wanted to, or was this another of *his* ideas? Had POTUS told Luscious to approach me in the Seafood Bar at the Breakers? Did anyone, anywhere understand my loneliness the way he did? As I stood next to Nova, I could feel my body language whispering, "Don't blow this." You could carve that on my tombstone.

HOUR 17:
PEACE IN THE VALLEY

Armed with a renewed sense of purpose, I took up temporary quarters in Norfolk, to be closer to the shipyard where Mondo POTUS was being born. My high-rise apartment overlooked the massive harbor, a crucial hub, where the world's empire builders had docked and done their business, indulged their appetites and slaked their collective thirst since slave days. Now, although the place was overrun with military technicians and shipping executives, it projected a holiday vibe. Dress was casual. Hardly anyone was in uniform. No less than a dozen brand name franchise restaurants and cocktail bars operated within two blocks of my building's blast-proof door.

It was a buoyant time. The first hundred days of Luscious's presidency unveiled a kicky kind of creative energy. I've heard new parents say the birth of their children gave them access to emotions they didn't know they had. Our new President and her virtual double had a similar effect on the nation's mood. This was certainly true when it came to Mondo POTUS. Now that POTUS was no longer in charge of running the country, those of us responsible for his legacy project felt like we were galloping toward the finish line. There was nothing more to chronicle or make room for. What once felt impossibly mercurial began to be contained.

I found myself spending hours wandering the multi-tiered hive that was the former U.S.S. Gerald R. Ford. The sheer size and complexity of it was stupendous. Its defiance of nature — for what on earth cried human domination louder than an oceangoing airport — was breathtaking. Though I tried, I doubt I ever saw the whole thing.

In those days, of course, it was a work site. Every deck clanged and sparked and buzzed. Lines of workers formed each morning to be patted down and eye-scanned before taking up their grinders, chop saws and torches. A space the size of a football field underneath the flight deck was turned into a multi-media production studio, where a team of software ninjas manipulated digitized audio-visual content with autistic concentration.

Veronica Tu channeled all this energy. I met her on the aircraft carrier's elevated bridge where blueprints and floorplans were spread upon drafting tables so large we had to shout back and forth in order to hear one another. Veronica was a playmaker. POTUS's lack of backstory no longer concerned her; she drove the project forward like a trail boss on a cattle drive. I grew used to waking up each morning to a barrage of her texts and emails, sent in those predawn hours associated with psychotic episodes.

Veronica's ambition was touchingly old school. Her sense of herself seemed inextricably braided with making Mondo POTUS a success. She believed her future depended on this a once-in-a-lifetime opportunity: "I'm not one of those," she said to me about the multitude of unemployed GIs (Guaranteed Incomes) she dismissed as "nobodies." Veronica wanted more for herself — and clung to the belief that hard work, rather than an end in itself, guaranteed material success and enhanced self-esteem. She ate her meals standing up and started using the kinds of steroids outlawed in professional sports. I found something poignant about her faith in what used to be called the "work ethic."

Del and Billy started showing up. "Duke," Del told me as we leaned into one another on the flight deck, our military grade rain gear shielding us from yet another whipping Atlantic drizzle, "you've turned a sow's ear into a silk purse." The flight deck was the size of four football fields. Originally intended to catapult jet fighters into the wild blue yonder by way of defending our trans-national supply chains, it was becoming a landscaped esplanade. "Thanks to you, this boondoggle has spared a watery grave."

That seemed unnecessarily harsh. I had come to feel a certain affection for the old girl — which, I suppose, is why I'm squatting here at this fraught, if admittedly pathetic, moment. But never mind that. If the Ford never became the warship the Navy envisioned, its engineering, construction, reengineering, updating and endless technological tweaks enriched defense contractors, rewarded investors and provided incomes for countless workers. Even bridges to nowhere make a living for someone.

"We're ahead of schedule," I said.

"That's good," said Del, "because Billy's eager for the Grand Opening."

Billy was below decks, testing the firmness of the king-size mattresses in the boutique hotel. After being informed (gently but firmly) by Luscious that she had someone else in mind for Secretary of Housing and Urban Development, Billy came down with the sulks. A woozy month followed, island hopping in the Caribbean with his "Buddy-Guards," getting loaded, heckling nightclub performers, shop lifting and taking selfies with startled tourists. Suitably worn out, he returned home, ready for a new distraction.

At first, the activity in the Navy yard seemed to help POTUS navigate the transition from President to President Emeritus. Once their time is up, Presidents usually flee the Nation's Capital. Johnson and the Bushes returned to Texas. Nixon and Reagan shuffled off to California. Georgia was Carter's retreat and Clinton took up residence in New York. Obama was the odd one, choosing to stay in the District's Kalorama neighborhood.

POTUS moved into an ultramansion with an infinity pool and a heliport near CIA headquarters in northern Virginia. A jetcopter enabled him to traverse the 152 miles from his backyard to Norfolk in under two hours.

Sometimes he visited us on the spur of the moment. "Pretend I'm not even here," he'd say. We'd call Billy (he came in handy after all) and the two of them would go traipsing off for the rest of the day, their respective security details keeping an obtrusively discreet distance as father and son acted out a private *rapprochement*.

He liked most of what he saw. The larger-than-life imagery on the walls, with projections everywhere (including the floor), replaying his greatest hits at home and abroad; immersive recreations of crucial events in the Oval Office and Situation Room; the moving sidewalk that literally carried visitors through a chronological history of his three terms; and, of course, all five Exbots — POTUS had his picture taken amongst them, flashing his trademark sheepish grin.

"I feel so old," he confided without a trace of Age Enabled irony. "Is there something we can do about that?"

I thought of Nova. That was her job.

"Let's talk." He tilted his coiffed head toward the bow of the flight deck and curtly turned his back on the gaggle of Exbots fawning over him.

People used to make fun of Nixon for wearing a business suit like it was his presidential uniform. One photographer caught him walking on the beach at San Clemente, as if dressed for a Cabinet meeting. As POTUS led me away from the animated memories of his love life, I realized he had adopted a similar style. He wore a blue chalk stripe suit with a red knit tie. He was no longer trim enough to keep the jacket's single button buttoned — I wondered what Nova made of that!

As usual, there were few preliminaries. As we passed welders fabricating the words INCOME FOR ALL in bronze, he told me he was concerned about how his children were being represented. He alluded to the depiction of Luscious's heroic fight in Illinois against the fresh water rebels. That was great, he said, but: "Is there enough about Wilhelm?"

"Well," I said, "Luscious is not only your daughter. She's also the President of the United States. And Billy is…"

"I know, I know," said POTUS.

"I love the mural of you, Billy and Luscious standing with your heads bowed at the Lincoln Memorial."

"Yes," said POTUS. "It's terrific." He was ruminating. "I'm just trying to keep peace in the valley, Mutz."

"Naturally."

He paused, as a phalanx of Navy jets roared lethally overhead. "And what about Nova?"

"Nova?"

"I feel like she ought to have a place here."

"Yes?"

"She's such a star."

"Oh," I caught myself shaking my head and nodding at the same time. "No doubt about it."

"I don't see why we don't make a version of her the way we have with my exes. I think it would be incredible if she could be the first thing you meet when you come on board."

"Well…"

"It would make her happy, which would make me happy." POTUS flicked me with a smile, "If you know what I mean."

"I'll tell Veronica to get right on it." At the time this seemed sensible. Like good manners.

HOUR 18:
HALLUCINOGENIC SPRITZ

Our maiden voyage from Norfolk to Salty Shores was preternaturally smooth. Weather along the mid-Atlantic coast reminded a few of us of life before the hurricane season became an all-year affair. Days were mild and breezy, nights clear and star strewn. The air felt soft as a satin sheet. We didn't hurry. The cruise took three days — time we used to test and tweak our various AI systems. For perhaps the first time in an otherwise underachieving history, technology aboard the U.S.S. Gerald R. Ford worked without a hitch.

Veronica Tu and I closed each work day with a light supper on the bridge, toasting one another with champagne cocktails from the hotel's bar. For Veronica, this was the Big Break she'd been hoping for. Another commission already awaited her in Lincoln, Nebraska, where real estate developers wanted the city's horizon altered virtually to display a seacoast on what they envisioned being its new western shore. She confessed to feeling nervous about being able to pull it off. An entire virtual landscape could be what she called "cheesy."

"But," she said, "if I've learned anything from Mondo POTUS, it's to never say no. Keep moving forward!"

"Like a shark," I said, slurring my words only slightly.

"So many of us live in fear," said Veronica, her throat becoming flushed. "Afraid of what will happen next. Rebels, viruses, storms."

"The shark of the new," I added, riding the crest of my cocktail.

"You're funny," said Veronica. "Change freaks out most people. It keeps getting faster. Del says history is the story of change. It's why Income for All was so great. It let people absorb change without having to constantly adapt. Our bodies aren't fast enough to keep up with what our brains say we're capable of."

"Veronica," I said, looking at her through my empty crystal flute, "you will always be one of the swift ones."

She frowned, but I could tell she was flattered. "Me?"

"You've been naturally selected for success." Fatigue was overtaking me but Veronica was jazzed and I didn't want to seem rude. It occurred to me we might go to the theater below decks and see one of the movies POTUS had chosen for regular rotation. *Breakfast at Tiffany's* or *Pillow Talk* — something I might sleep through. Veronica waved me off.

"You go ahead," she said. "I still have work to do."

Billy greeted us when we docked at Salty Shores. He'd been on site for two weeks, making arrangements for the gala, living on a diet of Long Island ice tea and fried oyster sandwiches. He retained his Eastern pallor in spite of the brutalist sunshine. "Thank God you're finally here," he exclaimed. "Between the go-kart racing and pee-wee golf there's nothing left for me to do!"

The boy certainly knew how to throw a party. He'd set up a private gala for VIPs three weeks prior to the public unveiling — a star-spangled extravaganza, chock full of champion athletes, multinational CEOs, military brass and swimsuit models of all genders. Golf carts bedecked with golden fringe ground dazed pythons into the asphalt as the parade of famous faces were helped on to the red carpet.

The evening was a mind-blowing avalanche, commingling the real and virtual to a point where — for this analog brain, at least — trying to distinguish one from the other felt like a waste of time. And wasn't this the point? As I watched the landslide of celebs embracing the Mondo POTUS experience, I realized I was witnessing the culmination of a cultural arc dating back to my Reagan era childhood. Politics and entertainment, accomplishment and fame, lasting value and immediate gratification had dissolved into one another like so much sugar water. Once (I think I was taught) self-government amounted to a civic religion. Freedom meant playing by the rules. A certain amount of corruption was expected, especially among immigrants (we saw this in gangster movies) but being caught in a lie really angered people. Then Reagan came along: a second-tier contract player who claimed he was a soldier once because he played one in a movie with Errol Flynn. What was true wasn't as important as what made people feel better. Kept them entertained.

Determining the correct protocol for the gala took almost a week. A lengthy discussion concerned whether POTUS should board before Luscious, or vice-versa. This was like assigning star billing in the *Towering Inferno* — which name came first above the title, Paul Newman or Steve McQueen? POTUS made a stab at what he considered magnanimity. He wanted Luscious to accompany him on one arm, with Nova on the other. Luscious balked at sharing her father with "his girlfriend." She said this could be "confusing" and asserted that, as President, she should make the ultimate entrance, kind of like the title card that says, "And Special Guest Star..." with the Marine Corps Band playing "Hail to the Chief." She had a point; in light of what happened later, I'm tempted to say she was prescient. Nevertheless, at the last minute, she decided to take her father's arm. After all, she said, this was "daddy's night."

The POTUS motorcade arrived at 8:30. Up to now, public contact between Luscious and Nova had been kept to a polite minimum. They saluted one another at ceremonial events, little else. If Luscious resented her father's newfound love affair, she kept it to herself. The demands of her office, as well as her health were top of mind. But something unnerving awaited her as she stepped up to the flight deck of Mondo POTUS. Nova.2, the virtual version of the woman on her father's left arm, reached out to greet her. Luscious would say she felt outnumbered.

There were speeches. Remarks, really. Everybody was on their feet and the tropic humidity, combined with an open bar and the aches and twitches associated with various orthopedic and Age Enabling procedures, made for a restive audience. It fell to me to welcome the many celebrity guests, thank the donors and say a few words about what made Mondo POTUS the repository of all things Exceptional. I cleared my throat and tried to top the self-absorbed babble of a hundred cocktail conversations: "Tonight," I said, "we honor a legend."

I did a little acting in high school — was a member in good standing of the National Thespian Society. Public speaking has never been the knee-buckling fear for me that I know it is for many people. But as I stood behind the microphone on the deck of what was now Mondo POTUS, confronted by that sea of upturned, prosperous faces, the import of our efforts shook me. I thought of Krupskaya, founding Soviet libraries across the frozen steppes in Russia. Of Ranganathan's dictum: that a library is a growing organism. It occurred to me that for once in my life, there was a lot I could say about where we were and how we got here — but I could read the room. Nobody cared.

I held a sheet of paper with the names of major donors in my over-caffeinated hands. I read those names, doing my best not to sound like a kid from Hammond, Indiana. Each name was greeted by a firecracker burst of self-congratulatory applause. The time this took seemed interminable to me, but the audience loved cheering themselves on.

"Mondo POTUS," I declared, finally summoning the nerve to offer a riff of my own, "will be a growing orgasm —" I caught myself, as a few offbeat titters arose among the few people actually listening, "Organism! A monument to our greatest President!"

There was a brief hush as most of the crowd ignored the malaprop I made of Ranganathan's metaphor. I turned around to see POTUS holding two thumbs up. Luscious crookedly smiling. Nova waving coquettishly. An almost glandular need to get the hell out of there — a feeling about to become all too familiar —jolted me across the finish line: "It is my singular honor…"

"Here! Here!" yelled a red-faced billionaire, famous for his chain of for-profit methadone spas.

"… to introduce a fighter, a heroine…" I decided to take a chance, to speak from the heart, if only for a few syllables, "…and my treasured friend: The President of the United States."

Luscious nodded perfunctorily in my direction as she positioned herself behind the microphone. Might virtual Luscious have given me a kiss on the cheek? POTUS, at least, patted my shoulder — rather like a high school football coach, welcoming the skinny kid on special teams back to the sideline.

Luscious, live and in person, had the crowd falling all over itself with joy but I hardly heard a word she said. I don't know who wrote her remarks. Del Capeheart may have lent a hand. I caught a touch of wordplay; punning tropes about fathers, daughters and the homeland, followed by an invocation of destiny and a joke about the family business. Luscious delivered her lines capably, though the stroke-like effect of her facial injury flattened her comic timing. It didn't matter, everyone laughed when they were supposed to. She closed with a flourish, promising to build upon her father's legacy — "an America, where everybody gets what's coming to them!"

The ovation for POTUS probably got the attention of sharks prowling in the dockside shallows. Never have I seen so many rich people surrender themselves to such a public show of ecstasy. It was practically Pentecostal. What began with shouting and stomping, soon morphed into free form dance. I saw the gleeful rending of designer garments. A man in a tuxedo actually rolled over on his back and wiggled like a puppy.

POTUS thrust his face into the spotlight as if its beam was filled with hallucinogenic spritz. It was the first time he'd been in front of a crowd since leaving the White House and he soaked up the adulation. "I love you, too!" he cried and the frenzy went on for another minute and a half (I checked my watch). After everyone was spent and all but lying in a postcoital heap, POTUS leaned in: "I hope this is as good for you as it is for me."

They loved it. They loved him.

"How about Luscious," POTUS extended an arm in her direction. "Madam President!" He pulled the audience toward him, "Don't you love the way that sounds?"

Cheers and laughter. Women, I could see, were wiping away tears.

"When they told me, 'You have to have a Presidential Library,' I said, 'What the hell for?' They said, "Because it's history.' And I said, 'History? We've been making history for twelve years! Isn't that enough?'"

The crowd started baying like a pack of bloodhounds.

"You know me," said POTUS. "I've never been about the past. I've always been about THE FUTURE!"

Even though I was standing back, toward stage right, I could feel POTUS's force field in my crotch. It made my stomach clench. Luscious, I saw, was standing at attention, her hands balled into fists. Nova glowed.

"Mondo POTUS..." POTUS let the syllables fall from his lips like super balls. "I'll tell you something. This ain't Chester Arthur's library. Am I right, Duke?"

His saying my name was like being splashed by a bucket full of ice cubes. My mouth twitched as if it was wired and my head involuntarily bobbed up and down, up and down.

"But seriously, folks," said POTUS, "we have a lot of great stories to tell and now, thanks to Mondo POTUS, we can tell those stories to people all over the world! As we sail the seven seas with this marvelous ship. But hey! Before we do that, what do you say we make a little more history?"

"Do it! Do it!" chanted some in the crowd, while others started calling, "Four more years!" and still others, "We're Number One!"

POTUS cackled. "I'm about winning, folks. You know that, right?"

The crowd chortled appreciatively.

"That's why, right here, right now, I am going to ask this lovely lady, this super Nova, to be my...super WIFE!"

Sound and light blew a hole in the humid night as Nova, sobbing like a beauty queen, toppled into POTUS's arms. Fireworks filled the cloudy sky with smoke and fire, the smell of black powder. Billy dashed across the stage, clenching miniature American flags in both fists. A woman (probably an android) in standard Secret Service garb tapped me on the shoulder: "The President would like to see you. Now."

A full-throated after party was under way, with revelers dancing to a Caribbean country-western band. I counted at least three of the Exbots — Juniper, Giselle and Ava — dancing with one another. Meanwhile, POTUS, with Nova by his side, held court, encircled by a privileged group of admirers who laughed at his jokes while uploading the moment for the envious delectation of uninvited friends and poor relations.

I followed my escort below decks to the hotel. We strode down a chromatically striped corridor (green, blue, red, yellow, black) scientifically designed to alleviate symptoms of motion sickness and stopped in front of a door marked with a number resembling a lightning bolt. The use of indigenous Alaskan numerology, echoing Elvis Presley's symbology ("Taking care of business in a flash"), was pure Veronica.

Luscious was pacing when I entered. She asked her handlers to leave. The room, a symphony of smoky blues and ivory tones, was on a dimmer switch. A single porthole revealed mountainous thunderheads being pushed in our direction by a low pressure system off the west coast of Africa.

Luscious and I stood apart for a moment, adjusting to the emotional gravity between us. Then she nodded and I stepped closer. Tentatively, gently, we embraced. She wore a blazer printed to look like it was made from mandarin duck feathers; something hard and rather sharp pressed through the fabric against my chest. Her sidearm. Like Eleanor Roosevelt, who packed a .38 Smith and Wesson when she traveled, Luscious now carried a loaded gun on her person at all times.

"Please Duke, sit down."

She appeared stricken by something. Her face was more pale than usual. Did I detect a slight tic? "Whose idea was it to include a virtual Nova here tonight?"

"That was your father."

"Do you know how she was programmed? Who did the work?"

"I'm not entirely sure." This was true. I generally steered clear of android engineering; I'm an analog guy: all I care about is whether or not something goes when I turn it on. My younger colleagues' absorption with how technology works means little to me. My focus, or so I tell myself, is on what it means — a quaint distinction, I know.

"The two of us — me and the Novabot — talked," said Luscious. "She said…" words failed her for a moment. "I mean, she surprised me."

I tried to think. Virtual Nova had been assembled at the last minute by an anomalous team. Veronica fumed about having to outsource the work; she'd lost a day hustling up talent she considered qualified, only to be told POTUS and Nova had hired a contractor of their own. Nova herself was then neuro-scanned for memories and personal anecdotes for the sake of authenticity. Del Capeheart may have been involved. He was interested in how doppelgangers might algorithmically enhance the archive of material generated by their flesh and blood antecedents.

"She told me," Luscious continued, "that we are sisters. Sisters, Duke. Do you know what that means?" A sob caught in her throat. It was like that scene in Polanski's *Chinatown*: Faye Dunaway bawling, "She's my sister, my daughter…" as Jack Nicholson's unstrung private eye slaps her — as if his blows will drive the unspeakable away. I couldn't slap the President of the United States. Not Luscious. But like Nicholson, I was revolted.

"This is somebody's idea of a joke," I said. "A sick prank. Or a rhetorical glitch! Sister-in-law is what she meant to say. That must be it."

Unseen lightning made a wiry, tensile sound outside. Luscious averted her good eye and lowered her head. She seemed so vulnerable; I forgot, for a moment, she was President of the United States. "Why did there have to be a Novabot?"

"POTUS requested it at the last minute."

I watched Luscious draw something up from deep inside herself. Saw the way her breathing changed. Her voice became level as an I-beam. "Nova planned this."

"Nova?"

"She's his girl now."

I called Del Capeheart the next morning. He and Billy had booked rooms in the hotel so they could crash without leaving the party. I told him it was urgent.

We met on the foredeck. Though Del wanted breakfast in the hotel's dining room, I was determined to get away from prying eyes and ears. I borrowed Veronica's ElectroMini and drove us west, away from the coast, where it appeared our spell of decent weather was about to end. The clouds we saw gathering during the night were closer now, darker and even more ominous. As I got behind the wheel, I had no specific destination in mind. I imagined Del and I would eventually come upon a halfway decent diner, like the one in *The Killers*, with its menu written in chalk and a waitress chewing gum behind the counter.

I should have remembered these places only exist in classic movies like *The Killers*; they're as out of date as happy endings. We passed acre upon swampy acre of palmetto plants, their fronds spiking the air like green bayonets. Alligators dozed in swales of fetid water on either side of the road. "I'm hungry," Del complained. "Where are we going?" He was a cold boulder in the air-conditioned seat beside me.

"Dammit!" I startled us both.

"What?"

We were the only car in sight. I swerved across the empty, oncoming lanes, making a U-turn and jolted to a stop on a scrubby bit of shoulder. For a moment, the endless exhale of the car's air conditioner was the only sound in the cockpit. I looked blankly at the palmetto sea — good for aging prostates, or so I'd been told. Mine felt the size of a ripe plum. I gripped the steering wheel with both hands. "Who programmed Nova.2?"

"Nova.2?" Del meant to sound innocent but couldn't help smiling. "She was a team effort."

"It knows things the rest of us don't."

Del stopped smiling.

"She told Luscious they were sisters."

Del closed his eyes.

Before meeting Del Capeheart, I had not thought about how complicated writing biography could be. I assumed it was higher power fandom. It never occurred to me, naïve as I was, that a biographer might come to detest his subject. I saw the battery in our idling car losing the power necessary to get us back to Mondo POTUS, so I got to the point: "Was Nova.2 saying she and Luscious were sisters supposed to be a joke?"

Del moved quickly for a big man. He opened the passenger door and climbed out, into the fading Florida daylight. "C'mon," he said. It was practically a command.

Part of me was still intimidated by Del. Having never been hit in anger by a man, let alone a man of his size, I was afraid of what he had in mind. Nevertheless, I swallowed my fear and joined him. Go ahead, I thought, feed me to the alligators! But Del wasn't thinking of mayhem. He was afraid the car was bugged — something else that hadn't occurred to me.

"That was no joke," he said, his eyes hidden behind vintage Persol sunglasses. "It's a fucking fact — fucking being the operative term." We watched an egret, white as a dress shirt, flare its wings and settle on a palmetto blade in the middle distance. "Mutz, do you remember the Rocky and Bullwinkle cartoons? Mr. Peabody's Way Back Machine? You're old enough."

Mr. Peabody was a long-eared dog with glasses; a scholar who studied historical figures like Socrates and Catherine the Great by climbing into a contraption resembling a port-a-potty called the Way Back Machine. It transported him through time.

"Let's imagine I am Mr. Peabody," said Del, "and we set our Way Back Machine to 2001. George Bush, Junior is the new President. *Gladiator* wins Best Picture at the Oscars. Nokia makes the coolest phones. And the Twin Towers are still standing in Manhattan — until September 11."

POTUS, Del told me, traveled to Nashville, Tennessee in 2001 to see the Georgia Bulldogs play Boston College in the Music City Bowl.

"That's when his long lost sister Merrie, shows up. POTUS thought she was dead — that was family lore. The lost twin. The part of him that could never be recovered. For a narcissist like POTUS, finding her in the flesh…"

Del let this sink in. The egret remained still on its palmetto blade.

"They became lovers, Mutz. POTUS and Merrie. Nova's DNA proves it."

"What happened to her — to Merrie?"

"Died. Opioid OD. Nova, their love child, was raised in foster care. She's tenacious. Finding her daddy became her life's work. I don't know who implanted this secret in Nova.2. It must have been an accident, something inadvertent that came through during her scan."

"Can you be sure of that?"

"Nova was afraid POTUS would never accept her as his other daughter. Never. She had to seduce him."

"He's going to marry her!" This burst out of me. "Does POTUS know?"

Del kicked at a tiny lizard in the coarse grass. "Of course not. But here's the thing, Mutz: If Luscious finds out about this, she may feel she has to do something about it."

"You know how much she loves POTUS," I said. "She'd never do anything to hurt him."

Del was calculating. "You may be the only person she trusts. Luscious needs to know it's in her best interest to keep this locked in the attic."

"Does Billy know?"

"Billy?" Del snorted. "The poor boy hasn't got a clue. No, as of this moment you can count the people who know about this on one hand: Nova, me, I'm guessing Luscious — and you."

"Plus the Novabot."

"I'll personally make sure she's scrubbed. Listen, Mutz, I want you to be very careful how you think about this."

The egret lifted itself into the cellophane air, its wings making like a check mark on the sky. "You're going to write about this, aren't you?"

I said. I was angry. I was powerless. I was disgusted.

Del pulled a handkerchief from the side pocket of his tailored cargo pants and wiped sweat from his brow. "Yes, I am, Mutz.

This is the biggest story since the ancient Greeks invented tragedy."

HOUR 19: (INTERTITLE)
SOMEWHERE IN THE CARIBBEAN

Meteorologists at the National Weather Service in South Florida scrapped the term, "hurricane season" after hurricanes started happening all year round. But the storm that hit us after the Mondo POTUS gala was actually a false alarm, a tropical depression that clogged Alligator Alley with eleven inches of rain and blew the corrugated roofs off old Indian River grapefruit stands.

It made POTUS restless. When we met before dinner, he was in the hotel suite he shared with Nova, admiring his custom-tailored commander's uniform in a full-length mirror. The jacket was double-breasted with brass buttons; there was gold stitching down the seams of his trousers. It reminded me of uniforms Andy Frain ushers wore at ballgames and circuses when I was a boy. He turned and gave me his best three-quarter profile — I was suitably impressed.

"I've been thinking, Duke."

In the old days, before he was President, I might have made a joke. I could get away with a little harmless levity from time to time, especially after a big success, like the NFL merger with the Defense Department. We'd share a climactic laughing jag. The intensity we experienced during these bouts of hilarity was almost sexual; I see that now. It's the sort of detail Del could have used if he'd been able to write his book.

POTUS was posing for me on a large treadmill he'd installed so he could exercise without leaving the shipboard suite he shared with Nova. The extra height made him a full head taller than me. "I'd like to take this boat for a spin," he declared. "Sail around the Bahamas."

Our public opening was in three weeks. Veronica's plan was to spend the next few days cleaning up after the gala and tweaking the exhibits. Exbot Harley (Billy's mother), for example. She performed diffidently at the gala, according to reports. And there was the matter of Nova.2 — God only knew how Del intended to take care of that. "Well," I said, "Veronica's still assessing the work to be done before we open to the public. We thought…"

"You worry too much!" POTUS climbed down from the treadmill before adopting a more fraternal tone. "Look, Duke, I have an agenda here. I want to marry Nova at sea. On the flight deck. Think of the pictures! When we return for the public opening at Salty Shores, everybody will feel like they've shared our honeymoon."

Trying to congratulate this man about to marry his daughter made me stutter. Unsurprisingly, POTUS assumed I was tongue-tied by envy and lowered his voice. "Not exactly the marriage we would have planned, Duke but that's life, right? Nova is a firecracker. Sometimes I think she understands America better than I do. She pointed out how, in politics, it's tempting to think a leader, me, for instance, is the one who stirs the drink. That's because I'm in charge! But if you look at all we've done — fixing the Constitution, winning a war, making people feel better about themselves — it was them! The people! I didn't do anything they didn't want. This job is all about permission."

"Permission," I said.

"I gave people permission to be themselves. And they gave *me* permission to make the country they didn't know how to ask for." POTUS toyed with one of the brass buttons on his jacket, the way Oliver Hardy might have done. "You know me, Duke. I don't believe in second thoughts. But Nova's made me wonder if not running for another term was the right call. For the country." He rolled his eyes toward the ceiling, putting his hands on my shoulders, his thumbs so close to my throat. "Time will tell, right? I want to thank you, Duke. I didn't get this library thing at first. But you gave me permission to build something I couldn't see by myself."

I felt overheated. The cabin's interior, POTUS included, began to flicker. I focused on his brass buttons.

"It's been a long journey, Duke. A long voyage. What do you say we take in a movie tonight? I have *Operation Petticoat* on tap. You know it?"

"Cary Grant and Tony Curtis," I practically recited. "In the Navy. A pink submarine. Nurses on board. Tony Curtis plays a scrounger."

POTUS laughed, "You're my Tony Curtis, Duke!"

It was at this point that Nova entered. She too was attired in nautical gear — bell bottoms and a chambray work shirt tied at the waist, with one of those white cloth sailor's beanies, the kind that make all men look gay, perched on the back of her head. After our interlude at the Air and Space Museum, I'd come to think of Nova as good news. We might have greeted one another with a companionable hug. Not now. Too much information.

Nova knew she looked great. On seeing me, she struck a chorus girl's pose. "Ready for a sea cruise, Duke?"

If I've learned anything during a working life providing service to others, it's that enthusiasm can make up for a multitude of sins. Be a team player! If that means taking a hit, absorb the blow. Carry on. Those in charge will reward you with, if not acceptance (too much to ask), their approval. When it came to Nova and POTUS, my capacity for enthusiasm had reached maximum surface tension. To keep myself from overflowing, I dredged up an old playground gambit and tried to make the craziness I felt sound funny. "Shiver me timbers!" I cackled, attempting my best Long John Silver.

"I told him we're getting married at sea!" POTUS sounded like a kid on Christmas morning. Nova looked at me, a little too thoughtfully. "You're coming with us, right?"

"He better," POTUS grinned as he wrapped a gold-braided arm around Nova's feline shoulders. "Or it's a long walk off a short plank, eh? These nuclear-powered ships are incredible. No need to refuel! How much life is still in these reactors? Thirty, forty years?"

"At least," I said.

"We could cruise for decades!"

"But then," I said, "no one would get to see everything we've created."

POTUS frowned. "That's true. And we'd need food. Of course, we could have it flown in."

"He thinks of everything," said Nova, kissing POTUS's cheek.

Del and Billy were braving high winds and taking a constitutional on the flight deck. Such a stereotypically odd couple — a lion nuzzling with a duck. They were digesting the news of POTUS's impending nuptials. Billy, as usual, was up for a party. He faced me with his feet firmly planted, a white windbreaker bearing the Presidential seal pressed against his chest by the insistent offshore fetch. Del held an orange and black Mondo POTUS ball cap firmly atop his head. There was a subtle shade of warning in his eyes. Billy said he thought it was a drag Luscious would be in Washington when the marriage ceremony took place.

"Well," I said, "she has a lot on her plate." Luscious had ordered herself flown back to the White House immediately following our brief but fraught rendezvous below decks regarding Nova.2. I had not heard from her, nor had I called since then. This incident brought to mind a story Del told me about Eisenhower. In 1956, Ike faced what might have been two cataclysmic crises: in Suez and Hungary. The first involved a double-crossing ally, Great Britain. The second concerned our Cold War nemesis, the Soviet Union. At first blush, both situations demanded a show of force. Yet either one had the potential to launch World War III. According to Del, Eisenhower played possum. Kept shuffling his cards until the various players grew weary of the game.

"It's possible Ike saved the world by doing nothing," said Del. Be like Ike, I thought, while showing Billy and Del my best shit eating grin: "I'm sure Luscious will be here in spirit."

Billy was to serve as POTUS's Best Man. Luscious, he complained, ought to be his dad's Maid of Honor. The three of us stood there, avoiding eye contact, until Del said: "I don't think that would be such a great idea."

Billy scowled.

"Remember," Del hastened to add, "your sister is now Leader of the Free World."

Taking the rechristened U.S.S. Mondo POTUS for what its self-proclaimed skipper called "a joy ride" was easier than I anticipated. Contrary to the old saw about the length of time it takes to turn an enormous ship around, the carrier could execute a 180 in less than five minutes — a maneuver that's coming in handy now, as I keep this boat turning and turning in circles.

A small flotilla of tugboats helped extricate us from dockside. Manning our helm was a sunburned former submariner named Burbot. Billy found him piloting an excursion boat on what had been Lake Worth, showing tourists the sunken mansions of departed Palm Beach billionaires. Since most of the carrier's actual navigation and seagoing operations were handled through various forms of AI, Capt. Burbot's job was largely for show. But Billy believed POTUS would want a captain and at least a skeleton crew to recreate the atmosphere of some of his favorite 1950's Hollywood service comedies.

The plan was to steer east of Great Abaco Island in the Bahamas before heading south, past San Salvador and looping back toward South Florida. Though radar showed a churning weather disturbance near Cape Verde, "Captain" Burbot was unconcerned. He said a storm like that could take a week to reach us, by which time Mondo POTUS would be back in Salty Shores and, as he so colorfully put it, "battened down."

The wedding was to take place on the flight deck. According to Billy, Burbot, as ship's captain, could officiate — just like in the movies. Things looked swell until Del checked online and found that the conceit of a ship's captain performing marriages at sea, as per Hepburn and Bogart in *The African Queen*, was, in fact, Hollywood blarney, with no legal standing. Alarmed, Billy turned to Del. "You need to get a cyber license through the Universal Life Church."

Del turned to me, a seasick look on his face.

"Mutz," he whispered, "I can't do this."

"It's simple," I said. "A guy I knew in college did it for a drinking buddy."

"Impossible! I've shaken hands with the devil in my time but knowing what I know, I will not be the one who declares a father and his daughter man and wife."

Until this moment, Hell had been an abstraction to me. But even I could see that knowingly uniting POTUS and Nova in holy matrimony tempted karmic fate. Fortunately, a small bribe was all it took for one of the unshaven drifters crewing for us to step forward. He was an older fellow, bearing a striking resemblance to character actor Walter Brennan — a detail not lost on POTUS.

As we headed out to sea, sending massive rollers crashing over what remained of Salty Shores' eroding dunes, I sat beneath one of the umbrellas on the flight deck and made a call to Luscious's private cell. I wasn't going to tell her all I knew; not yet, not over the phone. I just wanted contact. To hear her voice. Besides, I thought, sometimes the truth is overrated. I was thinking of Ike and the action of no action. But Luscious did not pick up and I did not leave her a message.

HOUR 20:
FOR LOVERS ONLY

You probably think you know what happened next. You've seen the news, heard the gossip. Looked at images of the happy couple as they accepted congratulations from the lucky few who shared their wedding day. Maybe you spied my face among the well-wishers — the bad seed who betrayed the trust of not one but two presidents by running away with an aircraft carrier.

The wedding day dawned humid and serene. Mondo POTUS drifted on the ocean's surface like the tip of a loving finger, tracing the curvature of a baby's skull. I was up early, found Del having coffee beneath a parasol on the flight deck. He reminded me that it was this part of the ocean, roughly speaking, where Columbus first laid eyes on the New World. "They'd been at sea for ten weeks," he said. "It was just before dawn. Columbus saw a light in the distance he thought might be a campfire. He said it looked like the flame of a small candle."

I wanted Del to tell me more — not about Columbus. About Nova. About POTUS. The wedding was scheduled for 3:30 that afternoon. After that, feasting in the hotel restaurant, featuring fresh caught grouper, jasmine rice and freeze-dried tropical fruit. Nova wanted to eat outdoors, but the weather forecast wasn't encouraging. Del directed my gaze eastward, where purple clouds obscured the rising sun. "Poseidon appears to have lost another round," he said. "In Greece they thought storms at sea happened every time the goddess Athena outsmarted Poseidon in a game of chance. She wins, he throws a fit."

POTUS was in garrulous form; his day started with brunch in the Call Me Crazy bistro. Nova was there, naturally, as were the Exbots (not including Nova.2), all of whom posed for a prenup portrait. It wasn't the kind of thing I would have done on my wedding day, but

Nova seemed to take it in stride. She beckoned to me as POTUS and Capt. Burbot repaired to the bridge. I followed her.

I was filled with dread, but what was I supposed to do? We entered the What Are People For gallery, a display devoted to the successful passage of Income for All.

"I have a favor to ask," said Nova, sipping a mimosa and pausing before a muted screen showing singing schoolchildren.

"Whatever I can do, I will." Anxiety made me swallow my vowels. This resemblance to the way Tony Curtis attempted to convey sincerity made me feel ridiculous.

"Will you give me away?"

I quailed at the implications of this double *entendre*. "What?"

"We need someone to stand in for my father. Since Billy is Best Man, I wondered if you would give me away."

I shook my head but answered in the affirmative — the same way Mike Pence answered reporters' questions when he was Vice President. "I'm sorry," I blurted.

"Sorry, Duke? Why?"

That I might have a death wish had never occurred to me. Just the opposite. I'd spent my career polishing surfaces and massaging sharp corners so I could lead a long, if complicated, life. Of all the artists I encountered in New York, Warhol, master of the skin-deep, was my favorite. Like Warhol, I cultivated a permissive naïvete. I couldn't stop myself from looking at some things, even when I knew they could kill me. Finally, I said: "I'm sorry your father can't be here."

"That's old news." Nova moved in front of another muted screen — this one showing POTUS making his "Every person is better than a job" speech at the Rock and Roll Hall of Fame in Cleveland. Bareheaded but wearing an overcoat, he made a chopping motion with his right hand. Frosty clouds came out of his mouth. "I was an orphan. Naturally, I've wondered who my parents were. But eventually you realize the life in front of you is way more interesting."

"Have you tried to find your parents?"

Nova pinned me with her eyes. "Why do you ask?"

"It seems like something many, er, people try and do."

Nova sighed. "I went through a phase. I dealt with it."

"Nova," I hesitated, "did you know your bot upset Luscious, I mean the President, during the gala?"

Nova frowned. "Is that why she left the way she did? Luscious barely said goodbye. POTUS wondered if she was having a relapse."

"Your bot told her — the President — that you and she are sisters."

Nova did a classic spit take. Tiny specks of orange pulp splattered across POTUS orating on the hi-rez screen. "Oh my God! Luscious told you that? She doesn't believe it, does she?"

"I don't know."

Nova licked her lips and touched my arm. "Bots can be like children, Duke. Mine was probably trying to affirm our bond. Not the right time or place — and a ridiculously poor choice of words — but kind of funny when you think about it. Thanks for telling me! I'll be sure to make a peace offering to Luscious as soon as we get home. In the meantime, I'll ask POTUS to call her. He'll set her straight. He always does."

The wedding ceremony streamed live around the globe. Nova wore a white Guo Pei mini dress. She persuaded POTUS to put aside his Captain Peach Fuzz uniform in favor of a hand-stitched linen suit by DeChirico. A rolling cocktail bar, bedecked with long-stemmed white roses, served as an improvised altar. POTUS and Billy turned their heads in unison to watch as the assembled crew made way for the approach of Nova and I. Pat Boone's version of Dimitri Tiomkin's "Thee I Love," the theme from *Friendly Persuasion*, crackled through speakers mounted on the bridge. Despite the clouds gathering overhead, everyone on deck wore sunglasses to shield their eyes from the subtropical glare.

I wish I could say I stopped this incestuous atrocity from taking place. Spoke up instead of holding my peace. Has anyone ever actually done that? Outside of the movies? Del Capeheart was equally complicit. But Del would have said he didn't want to become part of the story; he was there to observe history, not make it.

Bearing in mind that eyewitness testimony is famously unreliable, you can take what follows with a grain of salt. Here is what I think I remember seeing: POTUS and Nova exchanging vows (barely audible beneath the rising wind) then sharing a kiss. Del Capeheart's cloudy blue eyes, rimmed with red, looking down at me. How POTUS shook my hand in passing, squeezing it painfully in both of his. The bewildered look on a nameless sailor's face after he caught Nova's bouquet.

Capt. Burbot read a brief text from President Luscious, wishing the happy couple "every happiness." Wind blew what remained of the captain's thinning hair straight up as he held the white sheet of printer paper aloft for everyone to see. Then, like that! The paper was blown from his hand, spinning away, over the choppy waters until, like the petal of some flower, it was flattened against the crest of a wave.

POTUS looked happy. The reception in the restaurant was brief (the great ship pitching from side to side). He and Nova danced once (to Charlie Chaplin's sentimental theme, "Smile") and shared a slice of Key Lime cheesecake. Bride and groom then shook the outreached hands of crewmembers before heading to their suite, where an official portrait was taken. Someone posted it online — it drew upwards of 50 million views in little more than an hour.

Billy started feeling seasick, so Del and I took our drinks to the bridge for a better view of the impending storm. We found Capt. Burbot staring at a radar screen that looked like a psychedelic Rorshach test. Bright red and yellow were smeared across the unit's raster scan display. Burbot looked up and blinked as though emerging from a darkened room. He told us a potential hurricane was headed in our direction. Laying up in Nassau, he said, might be prudent.

"So how," asked Del, "do we get to Nassau?"

Capt. Burbot scratched his sunburned scalp. "Seamanship?"

Hurricane Yeller sideswiped us just after seven p.m., or nineteen hundred hours, in official jargon. Though the storm's main force passed to our north, it was prodigious enough to send anyone not directly responsible for keeping Mondo POTUS afloat to their relative safety of their cabins. I tripled my usual dose of Dramamine. At dawn, the view out my porthole revealed an anonymous deep sea mass undulating beneath a pelting downpour.

I did not know POTUS was dead. Or Nova. Didn't yet understand that what I felt as motion sickness was my world literally turning upside down. I skipped breakfast, stayed in my cabin and listened to Jackie Gleason's classical mood music, For Lovers Only through earbuds. I was beginning to feel more like myself when someone started pounding on my cabin door. It was Del, at a loss for words for once. He laid a massive hand on my shoulder and yanked me into the hall; it was fortunate I was wearing pajamas.

"Something terrible has happened," was all he said.

Billy was in the honeymoon suite, tearstained and blubbering. He raised his head beseechingly when Del and I arrived. Capt. Burbot was there, as was the paramedic who passed as ship's doctor. Del tried to comfort Billy. Capt. Burbot turned to me. It became apparent that, as far as he was concerned, I, as Director of Mondo POTUS, was in charge. By way of emphasis, he pulled me into the bedroom, to view the bodies.

Both were naked. POTUS lay on his back, like a boy in a meadow watching clouds go by. A silver sheet lay at a discreet angle across his genitalia, otherwise his flesh, now slightly gray, was exposed to the recirculating cabin air. Apart from the bluish discoloration of his lips, he was recognizably himself — only more peaceful. Grainy black and white images I'd seen of Lenin's embalmed body in the Kremlin came to mind; the slightly amused expression on Lenin's face, as if he was only pretending to be dead. Thus POTUS. Part of me wanted to touch him, to break the spell the way a caring parent might gently awaken a child in the middle of a bad dream. But I had never touched POTUS like that. Never.

Nova was on the other side of the king size bed. On her belly. Her head was turned sidewise into a down pillow, her profile obscured by a wing of auburn hair. There was less to see; the sheet covered her up to the shoulder blades.

"Nobody's laid a hand on anything," said O'Brien. "Except the steward sort of pulled the sheet over the President's privates." I randomly noticed that the captain was missing part of one ear; sun damage, I guessed.

"Stand back, please." Del was taking pictures with his phone, moving around the room on the balls of his feet, half cat, half forensic pathologist. He was documenting everything: The bodies. Clothing strewn across the floor. An empty champagne bottle. The treadmill. "You know this thing's still on," he said. We all became aware of a low buzzing, as if there was a hive of honeybees in the room.

A steward — part of the hotel staff — had been first on the scene. It seemed neither POTUS nor Nova had left a breakfast order before retiring. After repeated attempts to reach them failed, the concierge sent the steward, told him to be cautious. The kid was still standing by the open doorway, looking like he wanted to be forgotten more than anything in the world.

Billy blew his nose and tried to get hold of himself. "We've got to get back," he said. "We've got to get back to the mainland. Now!"

Capt. O'Brien scratched at the gap in his ear. "Could I see you on the bridge?" He was talking to me. I asked Del to take Billy back to their suite. The steward locked up.

I wanted to be the one who told Luscious of her father's demise. Was that the brat in me, or the lover? I was silently rehearsing my speech, trying to decide how best to break the news, when Burbot handed me a ship-to-shore screen. Luscious was on a secure line.

"Are you okay…" Her voice was flat. The tone wasn't solicitous; she wanted to know whether or not I was in a state, could be relied upon to do what she required. I quickly learned she knew at least as much as I did — that POTUS and Nova were dead and we were in a window between storms.

"Do you know how it happened?"

"No," I said. "The room is locked until we get help."

There was a pause on her end. "I understand Del Capeheart was taking pictures."

"Is that a problem?" I knew the answer to that question as soon as the words came out of my mouth.

"Look, Duke," said Luscious, "I'm going to need you to stay out there a while longer."

"Well," I took a breath, "how long?"

There were things she wanted me to do. She would tell me these things and I needed to keep them in mind, not write them down. I nodded, forgetting she could not see me.

There was a walk-in freezer in the hotel kitchen. Luscious ordered the bodies wrapped in sheets and stored there. Capt. Burbot, she said, would provide me with a small team of trusted crewmembers to help. They were to take turns acting as sentries, making sure no one interfered with the corpses. "We're treating Mondo POTUS as a crime scene, Duke. It has already been compromised. We need to limit the damage, right?"

"Right."

The full brunt of the storm was not expected to hit us until late the next morning. Before then, at 0500, a Navy helicopter would land on our flight deck to receive the remains of POTUS and Nova. Billy and Del Capeheart were to accompany them on the trip back to the mainland.

"Where will you take them?"

"That's classified." Luscious was curt, employing an executive voice I had not heard from her before. She was not thinking aloud or off the top of her battle-scarred head. "The chopper is also going to deliver something I want you to take care of. That, too, is classified. In fact, everything I'm telling you, Duke, is top secret."

"Yessir," I said automatically.

"Captain Burbot will bring Mondo POTUS back to Salty Shores. A full forensic team will go over every inch of that vessel. Everything that has transpired on Mondo POTUS since it went to sea is embargoed. I've ordered the confiscation of all smart devices— except yours."

"Luscious," I said. "I'm so sorry."

There was a brief silence. "There will be time for that. What I need now, Duke, is for you to keep this situation vacuum sealed. Not one prick of daylight. Not one molecule of air escapes."

"I understand."

"One last thing: Do you know the status of the Novabot?"

"She's with the Exbots in the charging room."

"Separate it from the rest. Keep it in a secure location until further notice."

Rain kept falling. The wind was relentless. Gargantuan waves began bashing Mondo POTUS. I found Billy and Del in the restaurant below decks, glumly nursing lattes and fuming over the confiscation of their smart devices. "How long until the chopper comes?" moaned Billy.

"Don't ask me," muttered Del.

I suggested a stroll through some of the galleries to pass the time. Billy covered his eyes. Knowing his actual father was dead and in cold storage was too much for him. Del took me aside. Not surprisingly, he was gaming scenarios in his head, trying to figure out his next move. He seemed desperate for a meeting with Luscious. "I have *got* to speak with her."

I assured him I could make that happen.

Del grabbed my sleeve, "She has nothing to fear from me! I want to help her. I hope she knows I would never dream of posting those pictures or selling them without her knowledge and consent. Never. I'm a team player!" He patted his brow with a monogrammed handkerchief. "I'm on her side. I want her to know that."

"Don't worry," I said. But Del was already worried — possibly for the first time since I had known him. Seeing him this way was like looking through the wrong end of a telescope. Though we were standing next to one another, he seemed to be getting farther and farther away. "She needs to trust me. I need her to trust me."

"Take care of Billy," I said. "We'll get through this."

Del returned to the table, where Billy was tracing his initials in white sugar from paper packets he'd torn open and poured on the tabletop. "C'mon, Wilhelm," said Del. "Let's go watch a movie."

I couldn't sleep that night. Kept shuffling and reshuffling through the detailed instructions Luscious had commanded me to memorize. I've told you my job is to worry: about deadlines and whether technology will work the way it's supposed to. Are the right people seated next to one another at dinner? Have sponsors been suitably recognized? Copy checked and checked again for errors? Reservations made? Diets accommodated? Rooms just so — with the views requested? Half the time you don't know why these things are important. That doesn't matter. What matters is that there are no fuck-ups.

Billy couldn't get away from Mondo POTUS fast enough. Del, I knew, was torn. Afraid he'd miss something once he abandoned ship. He told me as much: "This is like the flight back from Dallas in 1963. Lyndon Johnson and Jackie on Air Force One; JFK's corpse stowed in the aft cabin. They had to break the handles off his casket so they could get it through the fucking door. That flight must have been torture for Jackie. Like it would never end."

Warhol made a screen print of a famous photograph showing Johnson holding up his right hand, taking the oath in the crowded cabin with Jackie Kennedy by his side, obviously in shock, still wearing the bloodstained dress she insisted everyone in the country needed to see. Warhol smeared the image with lurid colors, reproduced it over and over and over again.

"You know," said Del, "people will be spinning conspiracy theories about what's happened here for generations. Shit, we don't even know the half of it yet. You're a witness, man. *I'll* be interviewing *you*. Take notes, for God's sake, so you don't forget anything. Details. I'll want details — and so will everybody else." Those notes, he said, could wind up being preserved as part of a special Mondo POTUS collection. And

Del said something else. Something that might explain why I'm sitting here now, talking into this recorder until my voice gives out: "You're gonna be telling this story for the rest of your goddamn life."

It was after midnight when I pulled on my shoes and went to the kitchen. I told myself I was hungry, but I wasn't hungry. I wanted to see POTUS. There was no one around. I felt the ship's nuclear-powered susurrus under my feet and between my ears. It was like being in a cathedral made of neoprene and steel.

A sailor, assigned to keep watch, dozed at a café table in the restaurant. He wore a sidearm in a holster buckled at his waist; a black xenon flashlight was standing upright in front of his bowed head. I coasted by him, quiet as falling snow.

An Amerikooler walk-in freezer was located adjacent to the food preparation area in the kitchen. It was a big silver box with a sturdy door that gasped when opened and closed with a terminal thump. When I cracked it, cold air made the pores on my face sting. POTUS and Nova had been laid side-by-side on folding cots taking up half the available floor space. They were shrouded in king-size bed sheets, their contours softened by a frigid blue cloud.

What I had hoped might be a sentimental moment of communion felt more like an outtake from *The Thing*, Howard Hawks's 1951 sci-fi movie about Arctic terror. The bodies beneath those bedsheet shrouds were still as fallen trees. I shuddered and stepped back, afraid of being locked in and freeze-dried like a Pharoah's hound at my master's feet.

Mourning was suddenly irrelevant. The POTUS I'd served was now on the glide path to becoming a permanent part of America's dream life. Lying there in that freezer, he was no more available to me than John F. Kennedy was to Jackie in the busted casket they flew back from Dallas in 1963.

HOUR 21:
LANDFALL

Last night, as I was beginning this story — with Mondo POTUS cutting watery donuts atop an ever-rising sea — I thought again of Krupskaya, librarian of the Russian Revolution. "We should try to link our personal lives with the cause for which we struggle…" Her words were so prescient! I mean, look at me! Separating the personal from the POTUS in *my* life isn't just impossible, it is pointless.

The Sikorsky Super Stallion helicopter arrived at exactly 5:00 a.m. (civilian time). It was a beast, able to carry more than 50 people or up to 30,000 pounds of cargo. A team of shock troops — Navy Seals and Marine Raiders — spurted down a rearward gangplank, crouching beneath the blast of the rotor blades. They were thoroughly prepped. The few of us ostensibly there to greet them were brushed aside as they began executing Luscious's orders.

They knew exactly where the kitchen was. It took just seconds for them to reach the Amerikooler, remove the frozen remains of POTUS and Nova and, carrying them like planks, transfer them both to a refrigeration unit aboard the Super Stallion.

On deck, Billy and Del leaned into one another beside a shambolic pile of luggage. They shielded their faces from the helicopter's heavy air as troops in dark-visored helmets and bullet-proof vests formed a bucket brigade to stow their bags. Billy turned to me. His eyes were swollen, the side of his mouth quivering. He held out his hand. I shouted to him through the chopper noise: "I'll see you in D.C.!" He waved before allowing himself to be hustled away. Del nodded in that knowing way of his as he climbed through the Stallion's side door. It was the last time I saw those two alive.

As Billy and Del entered the helicopter, six soldiers came down the ramp in back, carrying a casket wrapped in stretch camouflage. Another soldier indicated I should follow. We quick-marched below decks to what had been the honeymoon suite. The pallbearers placed the casket on the king-size bed; one of them pulled the fabric away and someone opened the lid. An alarmingly lifelike simulacrum of POTUS rested inside. The shock of seeing him this way made me scarcely aware of the soldiers exiting the room.

POTUS's hands were crossed upon his chest. He appeared to be sleeping, or deep in a meditative state. I peered down at him. As air moving through the room's ventilation system came in contact with his flesh — or surface area — it subtly began to soften. The corners of his mouth flickered. The effect startled me and I inadvertently spoke: "POTUS?" The gray eyes blinked.

"Mutz."

I passed my hand over its eyes the way I'd seen undertakers do it in the movies. Then I shut the casket's hatch and got the hell out of there.

It was later, in the restaurant, that Capt. Burbot found me, like Bogart in *Casablanca*, sitting alone with a bottle of Calvados. He was looking at the bottle, not at me, when he reported that Mondo POTUS had received a message from the mainland: The Sikorsky Super Stallion had inexplicably crashed, been lost at sea. Its stygian cargo and all aboard — Billy, Del, everyone — were missing and presumed dead. The ferocity of the weather made search and rescue impossible.

I felt the restaurant's striped color scheme, designed by Veronica Tu to ameliorate the effects of seasickness, drain away. Capt. Burbot looked like he'd been filmed in black and white. I pushed the bottle across the table; he grabbed it by the neck and drank.

Have you ever heard a tree fall in a forest? Believe me, it makes a sound. First, there's a crack, like a rifle shot. Then you hear weight, the slow accumulation of years, come crashing to the ground, burying the air that fed it. I heard a red oak fall at Camp David once — I thought the Venezuelans were attacking. After he finished drinking, Capt. Burbot let his arm holding the Calvados bottle drop to his side. It knocked dully against his baggy dungarees. "Can we go home now?"

As if I was making the decisions.

Capt. Burbot returned to the bridge — the same refuge I've chosen for all these hours in order to tell this story. Before my voice gives out. Before my wife's assassins catch up with me. I know this: Capt. Burbot and his crew no longer walk among us. Having served their purpose, they, like so many used-up Christmas trees, have been reduced to mulch — unless their remains are resting in some hazardous waste dump. The last I saw them, they were being greeted at the dock by a squad of Luscious's personal guard, elite maneaters fully outfitted with darkened visors and patent leather combat boots. Everyone was taken away in a black bus. Everyone but me.

I did not linger in Salty Shores. After Mondo POTUS made its surreptitious landfall, I was escorted back to Washington, D.C., where I tried to ready myself for whatever Luscious wanted. By now the seam joining my personal life and (as per Krupskaya) the cause for which I struggled felt as if it had been struck by lightning. Reality and illusion were mortally permeable. I was instructed to stay put in my Dorchester House apartment until further notice. To pass the time I strapped on kneepads and buffed the place's old parquet floors with a dish towel I'd pilfered from the White House mess. Evenings I re-read favorite bits of Nancy Drew.

I made a point of avoiding the news, so I missed the official coverage of Mondo POTUS's stage-managed homecoming. How what appeared to be POTUS and Nova were greeted by the rich and famous delegation selected to welcome them dockside as they stepped ashore. Or the way the POTUSbot that blinked at me in the honeymoon suite used the occasion to praise his daughter's executive ability: "I sleep like a baby every night. Like a good baby, if you know what I mean! Luscious is a star — and everybody in the world knows it." It wasn't until later that I saw the images of he and the Novabot, behind the bulletproof windscreen of their levitating jetcopter, waving as they took off to what promised to be a boffo post-presidency.

Love and fear have always been like yin and yang to me. It seems

I can't have one without the other. If Luscious was the sun, being an unobtrusive moon, minding its own business at her light's farthest reach, now seemed like a smart, if tenuous strategy. The mortality rate suddenly afflicting POTUS World made my zero degree of separation from the inner circle a hazard to my health. Resistance, however, was futile. I got down on my knees and rubbed lemon-scented oil into my apartment's floors. If Luscious wanted me purged, perhaps I could consider that a favor. I awaited her call.

She said she'd been thinking about me — words I received with some trepidation. Luscious must have sensed my nervousness because she was quick to add, "I miss our Nancy Drew. I try reading by myself at bedtime, but it's not the same. I lie awake with a million thoughts screaming through my brain."

"Don't you mean streaming?"

"No, Duke. Screaming. My thoughts. That's what they do."

"Well," I said, looking out my kitchen window at night settling across 16th street on Meridian Hill Park, "that's lousy."

"I was wondering," she said, "if you'd come over. Let me make you — I mean let my valet Cedric make you — a Luscious cocktail. Remember those?"

The sound of her voice, the ingenuous, almost bashful way she extended this invitation, made me feel like the teenager I never was. Like summer vacations and driving with the top down. Flirting with the lifeguard at the park district pool. So I shaved, pulled on a blazer and a pressed pair of chinos. Downstairs a black Yakuza SUV, the type Luscious favored, was waiting to take me to the White House.

Did I think I was being "taken for a ride," like some sap in one of George Raft's gangster movies? The thought crossed my mind — especially when I laid eyes on the driver. He wore night vision goggles and the double-breasted black moto-style uniform of Luscious's personal guard, her orchid patch logo stitched over his right bicep. The man's head looked like it had been cut from a limestone quarry. His hands, dutifully set at 10 and 2 on the steering wheel, were the size of NFL footballs. I didn't doubt his ability to make me disappear, if that was his assignment. But there was nothing out-of-the-way about the route he chose to Pennsylvania Avenue and by the time we turned into the White House driveway, past the familiar triple-layer repulsion walls and barbed wire, I was almost able to relax.

Luscious met me in the Oval Office. She got up from behind the Resolute Desk as I entered. It was good to see by her cockeyed smile that this, truly, was her and not some doppelganger. "Please Duke," she said, indicating the Googie-style suburban livingroom ensemble she had installed for personal meetings with celebrities and other dignitaries, "make yourself comfortable."

She wore high-performance red leggings and a black tunic with diagonal zips. The Presidential seal was embroidered over her heart. I must admit the way she kicked off her flats and (albeit with some difficulty) folded her legs beneath herself on the couch beside me was disarming. Like the Luscious I first met at the Breakers. Following a somewhat awkward pause, she asked, "How did Mondo POTUS survive the storm?"

A chrome cocktail shaker, beaded with condensation, sat beside a pair of frosted tumblers on a boomerang-shaped coffee table. As I tried to consider the implications of Luscious's question, I managed to overcome a slight tremor and poured drinks for us both. "It needs a little TLC but no serious harm done. I don't know how, but we made it through."

"I imagine you're anxious to get back."

I shook my head, "Actually, I'm still trying to process everything that's happened."

"A little PTSD maybe?"

"A little."

"We all have it," she said. I wondered whom she meant by "we." So many of us were dead. "I hope I can speak freely with you, Duke. You, of all people."

I tried to be reassuring, "I understand," I said.

Luscious daubed her weepy eye with a White House cocktail napkin. "I think Mondo POTUS is fantastic. I only hope someone will create something like that for *me* someday."

"Don't put it on a boat," I said, witlessly trying to lighten the mood.

"I loved my father," said Luscious. The reconstructive work on her face suggested chronic incredulity. I wasn't sure at first whether what she told me was a confession or a rhetorical flourish.

"I can't imagine my life without him," I admitted.

"Yes," said Luscious. "He made it possible for so many of us to be successful. Look at me, I'm Exhibit A."

"I don't know how you do it."

"What's that?"

"Carry on."

Luscious set her glass back on the table; she hadn't taken a sip. "Daddy taught me. He taught me to lead, Duke. It hasn't been easy. Luckily, I was born to it. And encouraged. Encouragement is so important. If there's one thing I can do as a leader, it's to encourage people, Americans, to be the best they can be with what we've given them." She watched me like a one-eyed hawk.

Contrary to what I had just told Luscious, I did not understand anything. Not what had taken place aboard Mondo POTUS. To POTUS. Or Nova. Not to Billy or Del or Capt. Burbot and his crew. These secrets were so big and so close, I felt them the way people with lost limbs say they feel their missing arms and legs. Luscious must have sensed how disoriented I was because she reached over and touched my hand. "What is it, Duke? You look like you've seen a ghost."

"I've seen lots of ghosts!"

She nodded.

"Secrets are so hard to keep," I said. "Aren't you afraid people will find out…about everything that's happened?"

Luscious looked at me with what I once might have thought was care. "I suppose so. Someday. But by then it won't make any difference.

It hardly matters now. People didn't mind when my bot campaigned for President. They liked having another me. This morning I did a face-to-face with Daddy and Nova. It's like they never left! They're fine. I'm even beginning to like Nova — we have so much in common."

I swallowed all of my drink. "Luscious, I'm afraid…"

"That's good!" she exclaimed. "It's how I've been for years! I used to think there was something wrong with me. But being afraid isn't a bad thing. It's what makes America great! Daddy knew. Managing fear. That's the President's most important job."

It was hard not to be moved by her enthusiasm. I thought of how far Luscious had traveled. What she had overcome. "Did you fear POTUS?"

She laughed. "Did I! I feared not being enough for him. I feared not pleasing him. I feared making him angry. But that's the point, Duke. I made it! I'm here. The only one left — besides you."

The curtains were open on either side of the window backing the Resolute Desk. I could see ourselves, Luscious and I, reflected in the panes of fortified glass. It occurred to me that I was still bot-less. Without a double of my own. Lillian Gish came to mind, floating helplessly by herself on an ice floe toward a waterfall in *Way Down East*. I longed for another drink. The cocktail shaker was sweating, making a small dark puddle on the boomerang tabletop. I refrained from taking hold of it with my own sweaty palm; I was afraid it would slip from my grasp and make a mess.

"Duke, all that matters is what happens next," said Luscious. "It reminds me of Nancy Drew. You see? I haven't forgotten what we read!"

I blinked my Age Enabled eyes. "Tell me," I said. "What happens next?"

Luscious stood unsteadily. It appeared that one of her legs had gone to sleep beneath her. She waited a moment for the circulation to return and then she stretched. The Leader of the Free World may once have been wounded but she looked every inch a tigress. "I've been remembering something about Daddy," she said. "I think he was right."

"About what?"

"About me marrying you."

There's a scene everyone remembers from the sword and sandal epic *Spartacus*. They know it, even if they haven't seen the movie, because it has been parodied countless times. Kirk Douglas plays Spartacus, the leader of a slave rebellion in ancient Rome. He and Tony Curtis, who plays the poet Antoninus as if his character had a Bronx accent, are chained to one another after suffering a bloody defeat on the battlefield. The Roman General, Crassus (a reptilian Laurence Olivier), tells the defeated slaves they will not be crucified, provided they hand over their leader, the one called Spartacus.

Cut to a close-up of Kirk Douglas, summoning the nerve to surrender himself. But before he can open his mouth, up jumps Tony Curtis, proclaiming, "I am Spartacus!" Then another slave calls out that he is Spartacus, and another, and another, and so on. It's a stirring bit, epitomizing selflessness, brotherhood, loyalty — which, I guess, is why it has been so easy to satirize. It's funny: Tony Curtis appeared in *Spartacus* only a year after he made *Operation Petticoat*.

Luscious stared down at me. "I want us to get married."

"I am *Antoninus*," I thought. "When?" is what I said.

THE END

ACKNOWLEDGMENTS

This novel was years in the making. It started as an idea that made people laugh in rueful recognition and, gradually, grew from there. Thanks to Dale Dassonville, Charlie and Carol Ward, Joe Vuskovich, Jim Poyser, Patricia Wildhack, Duncan Alney, Randy Starks, Nancy Stephenson, Lance Evingson, Diane Nalezny, Jim Schaaf and Robin Walton for being among those who listened and provided encouragement. Thanks, too, to those who generously read the manuscript in various stages: William O'Rourke, Michael Martone and Graham Hoppe. Brian Berlinger was one who read it twice. Brian's enthusiasm became the basis for a collaboration we had been seeking since we were in high school together, just starting out. I am grateful we found this project before it was too late. Mary Hutchings Reed lent her astute eye to the work in hand, as did Lora Fosberg of the Lubeznik Center for the Arts, whose involvement proved to be both crucial and truly compassionate. Once again, Andy Fry has brought a book of mine to life. Thank you, Andy for this partnership — and for advocating for Brian's creative legacy. Melli Hoppe, as always, has seen this effort through from its very beginning. Darling, you make it new.

COLLAGES BY BRIAN N. BERLINGER
(1951-2022)

Almost Next to Nothing
Work, Work, Work
Within the Wall
Within a Cell
Winter Kill in a Forgotten Village
A Haunted Village
Vox Populi
After Hours
Nightmare of a Thief (For the Ghost of Jack Black)
"Silence is of the Gods; Only Monkeys Chatter" –Buster Keaton

ABOUT THE AUTHOR

David Hoppe is an award-winning author, essayist and playwright. His books include *Letters from Michiana: Reflections on Lake Michigan's Southern Shore*; the memoir *Midcentury Boy*; *Personal Indianapolis*; and *Food for Thought: An Indiana Harvest*. Works for the stage include *After Paul McCartney*; *Our Experiences During the First Days of Alligators*; *Dillinger* and *Sacred Sands: A Play for Voices*, an audio version of which has been installed at the Indiana Dunes National Park. Hoppe lives in Long Beach, Indiana.

Made in the USA
Monee, IL
18 June 2023

36149486R00125